T0208288

Resurrected Gentry Crossing Over

In Nightseason One

MARGARET POOLE

WESTBOW
PRESS®
A DIVISION OF THOMAS NELSON
& ZONDERVAN

WestBow Press books may be ordered through booksellers or by contacting:

WestBow Press
A Division of Thomas Nelson & Zondervan
1663 Liberty Drive
Bloomington, IN 47403
www.westbowpress.com
1 (866) 928-1240

Interior Image Credit: Alamy Stock Photo

Scripture taken from the King James Version of the Bible.

ISBN: 978-1-9736-6264-8 (sc)
ISBN: 978-1-9736-6265-5 (hc)
ISBN: 978-1-9736-6263-1 (e)

Library of Congress Control Number: 2019907086

Print information available on the last page.

WestBow Press rev. date: 6/28/2019

Acknowledgments

I acknowledge that I was unaware of the depth to which dreams could go, until I met Gretchen. She was everything I wanted to be but didn't have the nerve to pursue. Chance would have it that we bumped into each other when we were at the lowest points of our lives—unemployed and alone. We both worked as independent contractors and so were ineligible for unemployment benefits. We left the unemployment office, dejected and not sure what to do next. As if reading each other's mind, we both decided to go out to lunch. Our lunches cost $16.94, which included tax. Gretchen had only five dollars to her name, and I offered to pay for her lunch, which left me with six dollars to my name. She became the sister I never had, and I her literary sounding board (affectionately called "Big Pearl"). I realized how much we had in common and needed each other.

My deep desire to be a writer had coincided with Gretchen's passion to tell this story, *Resurrected Gentry Crossing Over*. Finding refuge from injustice was our hearts' cry. My primary reason for wanting to write this story resonated with Gretchen's dream of redemption from a pauper's grave. Through her spiritual lenses, I met Bertha and Theo, two spiritual souls, who became her source of strength and guiding light (and also mine). I was drawn into the supernatural world, with Theo operating as the connecting force, bridging the gaps between dreams and real time. I was inspired by their great love and devotion for God, who was affectionately called the Creator, the Lord Almighty, and heavenly Father.

I acknowledge that *Resurrected Gentry Crossing Over* is the Creator's masterpiece, replete with possibilities and subsumed by unconditional love. I believe that love is the most powerful force to reckon with, even in dreams. I also believe that all things are possible.[1] Yet my desire is for the Creator's perfect will, timing, and absolute control over my life.[2] Unconditional love was, is, and shall forever be the amazing, eternal anchor and sustainer of my faith, fortified through my literary experience with Gretchen, Bertha, and Theo. In truth, where there is everlasting love, then real peace, courage, and strength shall surely abound, despite the odds. I've affirmed with Gretchen that we can do all things[3] through love, faith, and absolute surrender to the Creator's perfect will.

I acknowledge that I developed a sincere longing to be a part of the strong connection Gretchen had with Bertha and Theo. I was more inclined to be in their company—with them daily through Gretchen's thoughts, via her journaling. I felt safe and more passionate about becoming a facilitator in Gretchen's dreams. Her passion, willpower, wisdom, spiritual awareness, and resilience were inspiring and reassuring. Her unwavering faith[4] was infectious, and it gave me the will to persevere and believe in myself—becoming a bona fide writer.

I acknowledge that *Resurrected Gentry Crossing Over* has propelled my primary purpose as a thinker. It is a source of enlightenment, affirmation, and revelation about the Creator's amazing power and grace. It may help to bring more understanding of the Creator's omniscience, omnipotence, and

---

[1] Mark 9:23.
[2] Ephesians 5:17; Philippians 2:13.
[3] Philippians 4:13.
[4] Matthew 21:21.

omnipresence. The Creator's all-encompassing wisdom, power, and love transcend all else. The Creator's work of art manifested in Gretchen's quest to overcome evil and bring all into full awareness. Her plan for Bertha's redemption from a pauper's grave made me a firm believer that *Resurrected Gentry Crossing Over* is more than a dream or a legend. There is great expectation that it may bring redemption, peace, healing, and closure to centuries of evil acts.

Contents

Prelude

It was a bleak day in September 2018. Gretchen could feel the gloominess inside and around her. She flipped on the light to reveal a table lamp with gold fabric shade, red-white glass bead trimmings, and bronze pineapple base. A box of Kleenex was to the right, behind a laptop on a square metal-framed coffee table with a clear acrylic glass top. A chair with a metal frame and red-striped cushion, matching the one on which she sat, was at the opposite end of the table. Her slender figure was dressed in black slacks and a long-sleeve woolen fuchsia sweater with a low neckline, slightly exposing her upper chest. Her flawless, bronze complexion defied the sign of aging in a few gray strands along the hairline, revealed by her updo hairstyle. Yet her alluring brown eyes could not subdue the telltale sign of sorrow, and tears streamed down her cheeks. She reached for a tissue from the Kleenex box, wiped away tears, and started typing on the laptop keyboard.

"I have spent over one year alone in this empty house," she wrote, "and I'm just beginning to accept the reality. I have graduated to a Koil air mattress, and I'm more content with sleeping on the floor. My back doesn't hurt as much as it did a year ago, but it appears that the only end to my plight will be a pauper's grave."

Gretchen was experiencing another spate of unemployment, which she believed to be part of a diabolic scheme to ruin her life. She felt as though she was being taught the lesson that overachievers from her background have been made to learn. Her life seemed to mirror that of Bertha, a sixty-two-year-old spirit, but the detail was unfolding, only in Gretchen's dreams. She had met Bertha in her dream in 2005. Their ambition was always to strive for excellence in their professions as scholars and humanitarians. Many years had lapsed between them, after college, but Gretchen never stopped dreaming about Bertha.

Gretchen glanced over at the air mattress to her right; a forty-two-inch TV sat on a cardboard box near the wall of her otherwise empty family room. Then she looked to her left, toward the kitchen, displaying maple cabinets with classic crown moldings and a granite countertop, in immaculate condition. She sobbed some more and then began typing again. She had worked for only two months, and it appeared to her that this may be her last contract. Losing her lovely thirteen-year-old home to foreclosure was a distinct possibility. Yet she was thankful for excellent mental and physical health. She had realized that through it all, the Creator had never left her comfortless.[5] She'd been delivered from various forms of evil and given the will to live. She believed in angels and was thankful for them keeping watch over her all the time.[6] Bertha and Theo had been her strength and light.

Gretchen could see her world slowly falling apart and her hope dwindling away. She reached for another tissue and patted at her tears. Yet her faith was unyielding. In deep despair, she prayed:

"Heavenly Father, you've seen all, and you know all. In you I put my trust. Please, do not turn me over to the enemy, the tormentors of my soul. Protect me from oppression; save my soul from this perpetual cruelty. Thanks for granting me time to finish Bertha's story—our story. I promise to have it done before the next job comes along, or you take me home."

---

[5] John 14:18.
[6] Matthew 13:41.

Gretchen was inclined to believe that she must soon return to Bertha's former home, the Dreamersville Hotel in Dunkersfield, Gentry Cove. She got to stay there whenever she wanted, and it became her little home away from home, her peaceful place of refuge from tyranny. She felt safe there and knew she'd have a bed on which to rest. Interestingly, she found evil lurking around even in her dreams, and it was present also in Vanityville, Gentry Cove, where Theo and other God-fearing souls awaited their passage to heaven after a time of atonement.

Gretchen realized that her dreams had been taking her to a place where souls went to make amends[7] before their passage to heaven.[8] She'd been having dreams about Bertha since 2005. In the last fifteen months, since her near-death experience, Gretchen's efforts to connect with Bertha had been unsuccessful. While a mystery, it had been an eye-opener. Gretchen had validated her perception that Bertha was the spiritual embodiment of Phillis, seeking redemption from a pauper's grave. The epitome of evil in the form of Skip, an angelic fiend, had showed up in Gretchen's dreams. He had his being in Vanityville as well, and with the help of various cohorts, his connection with diabolic schemes had been undetectable for 265 years (in the Creator's view, that was a little over fifteen minutes ago).

Gretchen also realized that her increasing urge to be reunited with Bertha could only be possible through her connection with Theo. The void in her heart would go away only by thinking about him. Gretchen was starting to understand the difference between Theo, her imaginary guardian angel when she was in real time, thinking about him, and Theo, her down-to-earth angel when she was in dream world. She realized that he craved her company and felt excited whenever she was around. She wasn't sure why, and she didn't have a clear plan of how to handle the

---

[7] 1 Corinthians 3:12-15; Revelation 21:27.

[8] Psalm 66:12.

back-and-forth relationship, but she was learning as the story unfolded. She reached for another tissue from its container on the table and patted tears away. After rereading her electronic manuscript and making changes, she continued typing:

"I am convinced that I must follow the Creator's lead."

Then she was at a loss for words, like she had a mental block, so she walked over to the bed and collapsed on it, sobbing. Seconds later, she could feel herself being overtaken by sleep.

Shortly after, Gretchen could see Theo, wearing a navy-blue hooded sweat suit and white sneakers. She could hear the howling wind, rustling leaves on the tree and blowing things all around. As the wind quieted, she could hear Theo's huffing, his feet stomping as he jogged to the mountaintop. She watched as Theo's tall, athletic stature slowed and came to a halt. He drank from his water bottle and exhaled. He looked down toward Vanityville Inlet and its surroundings, and then up toward the sky.

His body shivered as he shouted, "My darling angel, I wish you were here. I miss your warmth and reassurance, but memories of you always keep me going."

Gretchen could see the glow on Theo's handsome face as his light-blue eyes watched the setting sun. She was happy that he seemed to be at peace. The only sound she could hear was the clicking from his cell phone as he took a snapshot of the sunset, a selfie, and other pictures of the mountain range, the budding white-pink cherry blossoms, and lush pine trees. Then she saw him put the cell phone in his sweater pocket and pull the hood over his silver-gray hair. He tucked his hands in his pockets as he began walking down the mountain and continued talking to his angel.

"I am three months late in celebrating your memorial and our anniversary," he said aloud, "because it's been a very challenging time for me. I miss you so much, words cannot explain. I feel so helplessly alone that once or twice, I used alcohol to make me fall asleep. I promise that I won't make it a habit. I'm not meaning to upset you, but I must admit that I've had deep feelings for Gretchen after Bertha disappeared and she came along. I agree, that's weird. Yet I never stopped reminiscing about us—you with me. Although Nate has been a tower of strength, he is preoccupied with his new family, so I don't get to see him as often. Meemee and our adorable grandson, Nateandro Jr., have been keeping him all for themselves."

Gretchen watched and listened attentively until Theo stopped talking, raised his water bottle to his mouth, took a few gulps, and then continued his rambling.

"I know you would love for me to move on, but I'm better off being alone, without any drama. Things always seem to go wrong when I'm around people. I don't think there is anyone else out there for me, but we'll see. For now, I just need to stay out of the limelight. My research project has been keeping me busy. I'm on chapter 3 now. Hard to believe that it's been ten months since I resigned from my job at the center."

Gretchen heard Theo sigh and noticed him shake his head as he continued venting.

"I can't get over how I was labeled a prime suspect in Bertha's disappearance. Though still a mystery, with no evidence against me, it has taken its toll on my life. Gretchen had given me a little hope but was gone after her outstanding performance at the center, which has been in shambles since she left. As you know, she had been the talk of the town for the huge success at the variety show. I must say, 2017 was the best year at the center, and memories of Gretchen still live on in the town of Vanityville."

Theo took out his cell phone and looked at it; Gretchen noticed that it was 6:45 p.m. Then she saw him put his phone back in his pocket and continued speaking.

"My love, I better hurry on home now, before it gets darker."

Gretchen watched as Theo started jogging along the trail again, and when he heard a ding, he slowed to retrieve the cell phone from his sweater pocket. She saw the look of surprise on his face when he saw her name on the screen.

"Dear Theo, I hope this text finds you well. I need your help, so I've returned to Gentry Cove again."

"Be calm," he whispered to his pounding heart as he texted back.

> THEO: Hi Gretchen, this is a pleasant surprise. Never thought I would hear from you again!
>
> GRETCHEN: How could I ever forget you?
>
> THEO: I could never forget about you. I think about you almost every day.
>
> GRETCHEN: You are always on my mind.
>
> THEO: I'm reassured.
>
> GRETCHEN: Did I catch you at a bad time?
>
> THEO: Never a bad moment in time or thought with you in it.
>
> GRETCHEN: I would love to connect with you tonight, if that's okay with you.
>
> THEO: I am on my way home from the mountain. If I could see you tonight, it would be heavenly.
>
> GRETCHEN: Take your time. I'll be waiting.

THEO: Be prepared to travel back home with me.

GRETCHEN: I am prepared. Drive safely.

She pressed END.

———⋄———

Later that same night, as Gretchen exited the elevator and stepped into the lobby at Dreamersville Hotel, she was all smiles. A joyful feeling came over her when she saw Theo.

He's looking so classy, she said to herself, admiring his burgundy turtleneck sweater, charcoal suit, and black Oxfords.

Gretchen could see the look of admiration in Theo's eyes as he approached her.

"You're looking as beautiful as usual," he said. "I am so happy to see you again."

"Thank you, and I'm very happy to see you too," she said, blushing a bit.

He quickly took her suitcase and set it aside, and as she walked into his outstretched arms, they embraced.

Gretchen could smell his aromatic cologne.

"Polo Black. Hmm, he smells so good," Gretchen heard herself saying.

"Thanks for inviting me," she heard him whisper.

Then she could feel his warm lips on hers as he cupped her face in the palm of his hands. They exchanged a soft kiss.

Gretchen could not hold back the tears, and she felt his gentle touch as he wiped the tears from her cheeks with his thumbs. He smooched her again. Then she nestled her head on his chest and exhaled.

"What unkind wind blew you here this time?" he asked.

"Unemployment and isolation," she replied.

He pulled her to his chest, and she could hear their hearts beat as one.

"I am so happy to be here," Gretchen managed to say.

"I am exceedingly happy to have you," Theo said.

She looked up at him and he down at her as they smiled at each other. Their lips met again, and they savored the moment.

"Gretchen, my Li'l Pearl, you've made me so happy tonight already, but will you join me for dinner and share with me what's on your mind?"

"Surely," she said as she held his hand and walked with him to his car.

After their late-night dinner, Gretchen and Theo cuddled up on the familiar beige sofa in his immaculate living room. They discussed being very lonely and not having family or close friends around for the past twelve months.

"I can relate to your heartfelt desire for change and companionship," Gretchen said. "I'm sure it must be very hard for you from day to day."

"I got beside myself; sometimes, I had to drink a couple glasses of wine to fall asleep."

"What?" Gretchen interjected, looking surprised at Theo.

"It happened after Nate got married and left home, six months ago; my karma."

"I understand. I cry myself to sleep sometimes, but I believe it will get better," Gretchen said.

"I believe it will. So what more do you have to tell me?"

Gretchen pulled the manuscript from her handbag and handed it to Theo.

"Part of the reason for my return is to get your expert opinion on this, our story."

"Our story?" Theo repeated.

He looked quite perplexed as he leafed through the manuscript.

"Yes," she said. "Our story, as in Bertha, you, and me. Please help me clear up the misperceptions and discord around us."

Gretchen explained that she had returned to Dreamersville Hotel to escape the cruel injustices she had endured. She needed a break from the constant deception, oppression, and bullying designed to break her spirit. She had been unemployed for several months and could see her life dwindling away, with no resolution in sight. She was fearful that her natural existence would end soon if nothing changed. Besides, she needed to get closure regarding Bertha's mistreatment and bring her the honor she deserved.

"If the truth is not revealed and tyranny effectively neutralized, I might suffer the same fate as Bertha," she said. "Life will go on as usual, with more innocent souls following the same path."

"Gretchen, I have no doubt in my mind that truth will be known in due course. The good qualities you and Bertha possess do serve to bring out the worst in your adversaries, while they bring out the best in you. In the end, all will be judged."

"Theo, you understand the situation very well. I could never survive the constant cruelty in a world that allows injustice and immorality to thrive."

"The cruelty you endure is more than what a human being should have to bear. Therefore, it's no problem for me to bear it with you."

As he stroked her shoulder, Gretchen felt relieved.

"I am reassured. Thank you."

"Gretchen, what more is there to know?"

She broke the brief silence with a sigh and then continued, "It may sound weird, but only you can help me in confirming Bertha's redemption from a pauper's grave. She has earned her place among the stars and does not deserve to be robbed of her ability to shine."

"I share in your grief and wish that we could have Bertha back. Yet I believe that she wants to see you happy as well."

"Theo, I do believe that the Creator has endorsed our

connections for reasons we may never understand. I have a strong feeling that we won't regret working together for good to overcome evil."

"I will review your manuscript, but I don't think I'm an expert at detective work. Please, be my guest and feel free to stay here for as long as you desire."

"Theo, I trust you and know you won't hurt me. I accept your offer. Thank you."

Gretchen felt at peace as Theo took her in his arms again, and after a moment's silence, he remarked, "Gretchen, I love you very much and would never think to hurt you."

"Theodorus, I love you with all my heart, and I am truly grateful for our friendship."

They could feel a thrill in their hearts as they smooched yet again.

"Now run along and get settled in while I get to work with your manuscript."

"I think that's a great idea; happy reading."

Gretchen could feel Theo's eyes on her as she made her way up the stairs.

I believe I've made the right decision, she thought.

Meanwhile, Theo's attention was drawn to the title of Gretchen's manuscript.

"Resurrected Gentry Crossing Over. Sounds very interesting. I am curious to find out how this, our story, will shape out."

He found the acknowledgments captivating and was fully immersed in the story by the first paragraph in chapter 1.

Chapter 1

Eleven months earlier, on August 13, 2017, Theo stood in silence while watching Bertha for a few seconds. He noticed that she never opened her eyes again. Yet he was content, knowing that she was still breathing, and he kept looking at her while she slept. He thanked Pattie for taking good care of Bertha and promised to be there for her until family could be reached. Little did he know that it was going to be a long haul. As he walked quickly toward the elevator, Theo glanced at the phone number and name on the card Pattie had given him.

Gretchen, I can't wait to meet you, Theo said to himself as he disappeared behind the elevator doors.

A few minutes later, Theo noticed on the speedometer that his silver Bentley was going sixty-five miles per hour as he listened to the global positioning system's voice.

"Continue north on Gentry Cove Highway, 115 miles to Dreamersville Hotel."

About an hour later, Theo decided to read a text message after stopping to get gas.

"Dad, I hope you will take the time to read this text and call me. It seems that you've given priority to something or someone else over your family's needs. Where is my dad who taught me to put family first and be ready and available to support them? You don't seem to practice what you preach, and your behavior is ridiculous, bizarre, and selfish! You …"

Theo heard his cell phone vibrating and noticed the name NATE on the screen. He pressed the green button and responded.

"Son, I'm sorry. Are you okay?"

He paused for a moment to listen, and Nate said, "I'm glad you feel sorry. Yes, I'm okay. You should worry about yourself."

Theo heard the ding on his phone but continued his conversation with Nate.

"I had to leave the hospital quickly to meet with someone at the Dreamersville Hotel in Dunkersfield."

"I know it's none of my business, but what are you doing in no-man's land?" Theo heard Nate's concern and realized that he wasn't pleased at all about his trip.

Theo explained that he had to meet with somebody who was related to Bertha. The feeling he gathered was that Nate and others believed his behavior was bizarre, being fixated on helping a strange woman. Besides, he appeared undisturbed when Nate reported that his home had been burglarized around 7:45 p.m. Nate had found the front door half-open and had attempted several times to contact Theo but did not get through to him until more than an hour later.

Theo listened as Nate continued to report that it appeared nothing was taken, but the prowler had left the guest bedroom window open. The image of a tall, slender person dressed in a black outfit with a hood could be seen on the home security camera. The prowler had escaped into the woods at the back of the house, and the police were notified.

Theo promised Nate that he would be home in a couple hours.

"Argh!" Theo heard Nate exclaim and apologized for disappointing him.

He realized that his apology was not enough. Theo admitted that the chaos had started about twenty-four hours ago. He asked that Nate be patient with him and promised to explain when he got home. Nate replied that he would not hold his breath and that Theo should not worry about him. Instead, he needed to get help before it was too late. Theo refused to say any more but felt relieved when Nate informed him that the police were there. He told Nate to be safe as he hung up the phone.

A few minutes later, Theo could feel the gratitude coming from Gretchen as he sat with her in the restaurant at Dreamersville Hotel. She apologized when Theo told her about his son's displeasure and the burglary that occurred at his home while he was on his way there. He admitted that his life had gotten a little topsy-turvy since his involvement with Bertha's situation. Gretchen could identify with Theo's concern and remarked that she was at a new turning point in her life as well. She could feel an increased eagerness to contact Bertha, her spiritual guide. Yet all efforts to reconnect with Bertha were unsuccessful. The more she tried to contact her, the more difficult it got. She became fearful that something might have gone wrong and decided that she must make every attempt to find out. Although it seemed elusive, her dreams had taken her to many places before, and she was prepared to again summon help from immortal souls, her only viable option.

Gretchen believed that her return to Dreamersville Hotel (on August 11, 2017) was not planned; it came on her unawares, the same way Theo had. Although this was their first meeting, she felt comfortable about sharing her experience with him. Theo looked handsome in his blue shirt, navy blazer, and jeans, which did not escape her attention. Likewise, she was flattered when Theo complimented her on how lovely she looked in her purple dress. Her warm personality seemed to make him feel at ease as she rejoined him at the table in the hotel's cozy restaurant.

"Compliments of Bertha. This place is her home, and I get to stay here whenever there's a need."

"Why does she live in a hotel instead of a regular home?" Theo asked.

"Bertha would have been homeless if it weren't for Dreamersville Hotel."

"I am so sorry to hear that," Theo said, making eye contact with her while expressing his concern. "Thanks for giving me this opportunity to know a little more about Bertha. How did you know to contact me?"

"I figured you would be the best person to tell me about her accident. I'd heard about you on the news."

Gretchen's attention was drawn to the TV, and she heard Bertha's name on the evening news. It sent chills down her spine when she heard that Bertha was in a car accident and saw her picture. Gretchen could not recognize her but had a gut feeling it was Bertha with the swollen face and bandage around her head. Yet she had a hard time figuring how Bertha could end up in a creek in the elitist town of Vanityville.

Gretchen noticed that Theo was listening very attentively as she played back the news report on her cell phone.

"Uncertainty surrounds the supposed hit-and-run car crash involving a victim known only as Bertha. She was rescued from a wrecked car and transported by ambulance to Vanityville Hospital, where she is in an unconscious state. A celebrity psychologist in Vanityville reported that he happened to be passing by and noticed a car on its top in Marshvalley Creek. The neighborhood police department reported that the crash occurred between 6:15 and 6:30 p.m. on August 12, 2017. A full investigation into the cause of the crash is under way. Anyone who is related to Bertha or has any information regarding her accident is encouraged to call 911 or the law enforcement office in Vanityville."

Gretchen noticed that Theo was very disturbed by what he heard. She was watching his demeanor as he listened to her explain that she had called and reported to Vanityville hospital and police station the same day about knowing Bertha. She had left her cell phone number with the nurse at the hospital where Bertha was admitted and requested that Theo call her. She admitted to feeling devastated by the outcome but a little hopeful now that she'd met him.

"I am so sorry for what you are going through, and I wish I could do more to help," Theo said.

"You drove for an hour to come here, putting yourself and your family at risk. I thank you very much for caring," Gretchen responded.

She did not believe for a second that Theo would ever hurt Bertha. She felt that he was one of the nicest, most caring souls she had ever met. As if reading her mind, Theo continued his pleadings. She could see the tears welling up in his eyes as she reached across the table and squeezed his hand. Although very tearful herself, she managed to maintain her composure. She was still a little confused and couldn't understand why Bertha had taken a car to Vanityville or how she had wound up in the creek.

"Believe me, Gretchen, I had nothing to do with Bertha's accident and a lot to do with her being alive. It may sound crazy, but I truly care about Bertha's well-being, although she is a total stranger to me."

"It doesn't sound crazy to me, and I believe you," Gretchen reassured Theo and continued to speak on Bertha's behalf.

Gretchen noticed that Theo was starting to feel comfortable around her. He could tell that she was feeling at ease around him as well. Theo showed Gretchen pictures of himself dressed in a gray sweat suit with a hoodie and white sneakers. She noticed he had an eagerness to play back snippets of events on the videos he'd recorded on his camera. Gretchen listened attentively and documented as much as possible. She anticipated that it would be painful for him to relive the moments but realized that he felt the need to tell her about how he became involved. She discovered that he was on his way down from a routine trip to the mountain.

Little did he know that a few minutes later, his life would change forever.

He zoomed in on Vanityville Inlet and then on the various shades of red, orange, and yellow-green pine trees.

It appeared that fall had arrived a little more than a month early, Gretchen heard Theo interject.

Amidst the howling wind that scattered leaves around, he could hear the shrill, raspy squawking of pelicans and the splashing of water as he approached the inlet. He stopped to take snapshots of some brown pelicans pouching up their supper from a shoal of pogies in the shallow waters of the inlet. Then he zoomed in on larger fishes—a couple small groups of striped basses and bluefishes swirling and meandering away in the opposite direction.

Gretchen followed along in her mind's eyes as Theo recalled himself hurrying to put his camera away; a strong gust of wind nearly knocked it from his hands. He had picked up on the hint that it was time to go. So he put away the camera and started jogging along the trail. He had passed the marina on his left when he increased his speed as the wind blew harder. About two hundred yards up the road, he slowed, breathing heavily, as he walked toward the bridge over Marshvalley Creek. Halfway across the bridge, he stopped to look at the twisted and misshapen metal rail, part of it shredded. He hurriedly took out his mini binoculars from the pouch around his waist as he moved closer. He saw a white car, upside down in the creek. Theo could hear his heart pounding in his chest as he quickly pulled out his cell phone, dialed 911, and reported the accident.

Gretchen listened as Theo recalled that his attention was drawn to a red pickup truck pulling out from the slip-road leading to the scene of the crash. He had caught a glimpse, in his binoculars, of the driver, a man with a beard, wearing a red cap. Theo reached for his camera, but he was too late. The pickup truck zipped past him before he could take a picture.

"I remember seeing that same pickup truck a few months ago, when I went to visit Colanda," he said.

Theo's attention was drawn back to the boardwalk; he heard a siren wailing, and within seconds, he saw an ambulance moving toward the accident scene. He then hurried over to the rail again, and moments later, he could see someone strapped to a gurney, which was wheeled into the back of the ambulance. Again, he heard the wailing sound of sirens and saw lights flashing as the ambulance left the scene. It appeared to Theo that only one occupant was found in the white car involved in the crash, and he prayed for a miracle. He recalled trying to avoid a few bystanders who had appeared on the boardwalk. He hurriedly crossed the street and headed toward Vanityville Municipal Park.

"Vanityville Police," he heard a voice call out to him. "Put your hands in the air slowly, above your head."

Theo recalled feeling petrified but managed to do exactly as he was told; he slowly raised both his hands above his head.

"Now turn around, slowly."

He turned around slowly and blinked into a flashlight shining in his face.

"Dr. Worlington, Officers Gabriel and Rafael here, with a question or two for you," Theo heard someone ask as he turned slowly to face two officers.

"We're kinda new, but we know you, Nate's dad, the celebrity psychologist," the other officer announced.

"I'm not sure if I would consider myself a celebrity psychologist, but I'm Nate's dad, all right. How can I help you?"

"Dr. Worlington, we need to know what you were doing tonight in Marshvalley Creek."

Facing Officer Gabriel, Theo responded, quite calmly, "I was not directly in the creek. Instead, I happened to notice a car in the creek when I was on the boardwalk. I don't know how it got there or who was involved. I was standing on the boardwalk near the broken rail, observing through my binoculars. I could see clearly, but in my gut, I felt that someone might be trapped inside that car, so I called for help."

"Well, you did the right thing, and your action may have saved the driver's life. What time were you on the boardwalk?"

"I arrived on the scene at 1840 hours. I didn't witness the accident; I only called for help."

"Dr. Worlington, where were you earlier this evening?" Officer Rafael asked.

"'Dr. Worlington' is becoming a bit overused," he replied. "You may call me Theo. I was just about to leave the mountain, where I jog most mornings."

He showed the officers the time captured in his camera as he responded.

"We'll keep it real professional, Dr. Worlington," Officer Rafael replied.

Theo, thinking it to be the appropriate response, concurred.

"That's fine with me. See, it was 6:25 p.m. when I took this last picture."

He noticed that both police officers were fascinated by the last two snapshot videos with the striped basses and bluefishes swimming out to sea.

"Do you fish?" Theo asked.

"Yes, we do," the officers replied in unison, which Theo thought was very interesting.

"Well, that video with the schoolie stripers was the last snapshot I took when passing the inlet," Theo explained, pointing toward the camera screen. Then after taking out his cell phone from his pouch, he continued, "See here also, I called for emergency assistance at 6:43 p.m. on my cell phone, and I saw the ambulance arriving at the scene about five minutes later."

Theo noticed that the officers glanced at each other when he mentioned another detail about the crash.

Theo felt it was important to mention about the driver in the red pickup truck he saw at the crash site, just before the ambulances got there. He apologized for not being able to gather more information about the pickup truck driver.

"You've done well, sir," Officer Rafael said. "We have enough info; would you send me a copy of your last video?"

"I'll be more than happy to email you a copy of it," Theo replied.

"We'll contact you if we need further information," Officer Gabriel said, handing a card to Theo. "Would you like a ride home?"

Theo gladly accepted; he figured it would take him another ten minutes if he were to walk home through the shortcut, north of the park. As the two officers drove him home, Theo began transferring the videos and snapshots from his camera to his cell phone. Just then, Officer Gabriel, sitting in the front passenger seat, made an announcement.

"Got it," he said. "My favorite game fish in the world."

Theo became fascinated and watched as Gabriel zoomed in on a fish.

"How old do you think this one is, sir?"

"That's about a fourteen-inch striper. So that'll make it about two years old."

"Pretty good," Gabriel exclaimed.

"The striped bass is one of my favorite fishes," said Theo.

"I can tell this one's a hybrid striped bass by the broken black stripes on its body," said Gabriel.

"Is the hybrid a cross between a striped and white bass?" Rafael asked.

"Yep," Gabriel replied.

The conversation didn't take Theo's mind off the crash site for too long, but he was relieved when the interrogation was over.

A few seconds later, Theo directed the officers to turn down the driveway of his white two-story house, located at 119 South Cove Estates Drive. For a moment, he felt renewed appreciation for the well-kept garden filled with red roses and other flowers.

Life and all its beauty suddenly seemed to have a little more meaning. He got out of the unmarked police car and thanked the officers for the ride, and they drove off.

A few minutes later, as Theo, in white polo shirt and black pants, was backing his Bentley out of his driveway, Nate drove up in his white Porsche sedan and blocked him in.

"What's up, Dad? What's the hurry?" Nate asked as he walked over to Theo's car.

He noticed that Nate was wearing his gold and black outfit. "What are you trying to accomplish?" Theo questioned.

"Since that should be my question, what's the answer?"

"Well, if you truly love your Panamera as much as you love me, get it out of my way," Theo snapped, equally sarcastic. "I must get back to the hospital, in one piece and peacefully, now."

"Sure, Dad, you've got my undivided attention."

"I'll catch up with you later when you return from work, and you'll have my attention then," Theo said loudly, "but you'll wish it was divided."

Theo's attention was drawn to Nate's flashing silhouette, as he hurried back to his car and sped away.

Ding.

Theo read Nate's text message:

"Don't try to catch up with me later!"

———◇———

Minutes later, Theo exhaled a sigh of relief as he sat down on a chair, facing the comatose person on the bed in the Vanityville Hospital's Intensive Care Unit. His eyes fixed on the woman's wristband; her name was Bertha. Then his stare shifted to the moderate facial swelling and bruising, mostly around her eyes, cheeks, and lips, and the white, blood-tinged bandage wrapped around her head. Theo watched Bertha's slow, rhythmic breathing. Then, his focus shifted to the blue tube connected to a breathing

10

tube in Bertha's mouth and anchored by a strap around her lower jawbone. The other end connected to a ventilator, and Theo could hear the whooshing sounds coming from it. Though difficult for him to watch, he realized that the peaceful look on Bertha's face had a calming effect on him. Amid the sorrow he felt was happiness knowing she had not succumbed to death.

I thank Divine Providence for getting me to the creek on time, Theo said to himself.

As his eye shifted back to observing the normal rhythm on the heart monitor, he noticed an attractive blonde nurse come in, carrying a bag of sodium chloride. *Mattie, RN* was written on the breast pocket of her navy-blue scrubs. Theo took that moment as his cue to exit, and the clock on the wall showing 7:55 p.m. confirmed it.

Theo walked out of the room and was about to leave when he was intercepted in the hallway by another nurse with red curly hair and looking cute also in navy-blue scrubs.

"Dr. Worlington," she said. "What brings you here?"

"Hello, Glenda," Theo replied. "Good to see you. I came to visit Ber—"

"Oh, I saw the newsflash on the TV, just as I was leaving for work, about an hour ago. If you don't mind me asking, what was she doing there?"

"I have no idea. Do you know h—"

"How did the crash happen?" Glenda interrupted Theo again. Her flushed cheeks indicated surprise to him.

"I'm in a state of shock," she said, confirming his thought.

But why should she be? Theo asked himself, feeling uncomfortable by Glenda's questioning. He regarded the nurse's behavior as inappropriate and avoided engaging in a conversation with her.

"No time to talk now," he said. "Sorry."

As he went to leave, Mattie caught up with him in the hallway.

"Hello, sir," she said. "Are you a family member?"

Theo stopped and replied, "No, but I am temporarily her guardian. How may I help you?"

"I just needed to know what family member to contact so I can complete the details on her chart. All I have is "Bertha"—the name written on a T-shirt found in her handbag."

Theo noticed Glenda come out of the room and approach nurse Mattie.

"I don't have any information, but please take good care of Bertha. I'll follow up about the details later."

Theo quickly walked away to avoid further questioning.

The next evening, Sunday, Theo was feeling comfortable in his casual attire: a navy blazer over the light-blue dress shirt tucked into his dark-blue jeans, black belt, blue socks, and black Rockford shoes. He could feel Glenda's brown eyes on him as he made his way down the hallway. Then he noticed Pattie, a middle-aged, charge nurse approaching, in navy-blue scrubs. *She's always pleasant and very caring*, he thought.

"The nurse I wanted to see," Theo announced as she stopped to greet him.

"Hey! How is it going, Dr. Worlington? I've heard about your heroic effort yesterday. Are you here to visit Bertha?" Theo could hear the familiar southern drawl.

"Yes, and I was just about to leave." He paused for second, then continued, "I see she is still on a ventilator. What's the plan of care?"

"I'm sorry," Pattie answered, "but due to patient confidentiality, I cannot say much about her to you, since you are not family. However, I will say it was miraculous that she came out of that accident alive. She is extremely fortunate, thanks to you."

"I agree, and while she remains in a coma, I'll be her surrogate until her family can be contacted."

Theo gave Pattie his contact information, and she promised to let him know how he may help. Theo's attention was drawn suddenly to Glenda, who hurried away from the nurses' station and into Bertha's room. Then, his attention shifted back to Pattie as she informed him that he couldn't do much for Bertha while she remained in a coma. Theo was about to walk away when he paused again.

With a puzzled look on his face, he mumbled to himself, "I have a feeling Bertha will need me to hang around a little longer."

He noticed that Pattie had a concerned look on her face as well, and they were both distracted by the announcement overhead: "Code Blue, ICU bed Room seven! Code Blue, ICU bed seven! Code Blue, ICU bed seven."

Theo watched from the hallway as several individuals, including Pattie, rushed into Bertha's room. He decided to follow his gut feeling that something was wrong and linger awhile. He walked toward Room 7 and stood outside the closed door, from where he could hear a commotion inside.

He heard, "Continue compressions," which meant to him that resuscitation efforts were in progress. Then he decided to sit in the waiting room because the event was too much for him to handle. After about five minutes, he dozed off.

Theo saw himself standing on the boardwalk at Marshvalley Creek, his binoculars zooming in on the figure of a woman near the crash site as he recalled the white car with its wheels up. The woman was dressed in purple, barefoot and running, breathing heavily, and in distress. Then he saw another figure in a hooded black outfit, flashlight in hand, chasing after the woman in purple. He saw the hooded figure closing in on her as she tripped and fell. He could see the bearded face of the figure hovering over the woman on the ground and about to strike her with the huge flashlight. Then Theo saw darkness.

Then, Theo saw himself sitting in the left corner at the foot of Bertha's bed in Room 7. He could see her legs twitching and heard a muffled sound coming from her as she rocked her head from side to side. Theo saw two other individuals in navy-blue scrubs hold Bertha down while Glenda injected something from a small syringe into her IV tube. Another individual, in green scrubs, was flashing a penlight in Bertha's eyes. Theo could sense a stillness in the room and noticed that the two individuals had released their grip on Bertha. Theo could see that she was no longer struggling but appeared to be sleeping peacefully, as the four individuals left the room.

Seconds later, Theo heard his cell phone vibrating in his pocket. He jumped up out of his sleep. He quickly reached for his cell and noticed NATE on the screen. He pressed the green button.

"Sorry, Nate. I can't speak now. I'll call back in a few minutes," Theo said, and then he pressed the red button.

As he entered Bertha's room, he heard Pattie reassuring her.

"Bertha, please squeeze my finger if you can hear me," Pattie said. "You are at Vanityville Hospital in Gentry Cove. You got injured in a car crash and were brought here by ambulance."

As Theo moved toward her bedside, he noticed Bertha's eyes twitching, and then they slowly opened. She looked at him for a second, and then her eyes closed again. Theo could see the peaceful look on her face. He was aware that Pattie had noticed Bertha's reaction to his presence and informed her that Theo was the one who had called for help and saved her life.

Chapter 2

Gretchen and Theo were both silent when the videos ended, and Theo had nothing else to say. She knew that reliving those moments were truly excruciating for him. She was also in deep grief all over again, after Theo's graphic account of Bertha's near-death experience that had left her in a coma. They could see the sadness in each other's eyes, and as they reached for each other's hands across the table, Gretchen could feel the energy, like warm heat being transmitted from Theo's hands to hers. She squeezed his white hands in gratitude, and they breathed a sigh of relief, almost in one breath that was audible to both. They knew at that moment that their meeting was ordained. In their mind's eyes, they could see their hands, black and white, interlocked in defiance to the evil around them, bringing their worlds closer.

They could see the bands of angels in a glorious array of colors, watching over them. There was no doubt that Gretchen's and Theo's hearts were in one accord. Gretchen felt gratitude, believing that Theo was God-given, literally, as in the meaning of his first name, Theodorus. She didn't know for sure who he was but felt an unbreakable bond with him already. She believed that the man sitting across from her was predestined to be the angel to lead her to Bertha and be their support system. This was like part of her dream coming true.

Theo was thinking along the same line. He was stunned by Gretchen's beauty, inside and out, and noticed how much she looked like Bertha. He believed that Gretchen was godsent also. The little he already knew about her was enough to convince him that she brought joy and healing to many.

"Theo, thanks a million for saving Bertha's life," Gretchen said, "and I am truly sorry for all the inconvenience to you and your family. Please give Nate my regards. I hope to meet him some day."

"Gretchen, I appreciate your kindness. Bertha is not an inconvenience to my family. I haven't been able to explain it all to Nate. I'll make it up to him soon."

Gretchen watched as Theo drank a few sips of water. Then he wanted to know more about her relationship with Bertha. He felt that this was an opportunity to view things about Bertha through Gretchen's lenses. Gretchen was concerned that it may take up too much of his time, but Theo insisted.

"Please tell me a little about Bertha's background, like where was she from. How did you meet her?"

"We know little about Bertha," she said, "but she endured a lot of suffering throughout her life. We don't know any details about her childhood."

She thought for a moment and then continued to speak.

"I met Bertha twelve years ago in a dream, so I thought, on August 25, 2005, after going to bed feeling very sad and lonely."

Gretchen recalled that she was walking aimlessly in a marshland and ended up at a little old house with a rusting zinc roof. She saw a woman sitting on a bench in the yard, a few feet from the dirt road where she stood. Gretchen felt as if she was looking at herself, except the woman had a short, curly Afro partially covered by a bonnet. Her bronze and flawless complexion was radiant. Her beautiful white teeth would make the world smile back when she smiled, and the twinkle in her dark-brown eyes was invigorating. Gretchen noticed also that Bertha was wearing a purple-and-white floral cotton dress, ankle-length, with half-sleeves and a white apron.

Gretchen was not startled by this person, because she appeared very friendly, smiling as she beckoned for her to come over. So Gretchen walked over and sat beside her.

"You must be Gretchen, my Li'l Pearl. I was praying and hoping you would come."

Gretchen felt a little queasy but managed to maintain her composure.

"Please refresh my memory," she said, smiling back at the woman.

"I am Bertha, the name given to me when I got here."

"From where?"

"I don't really know from where or how or when, but the Creator knows," Bertha replied.

Gretchen decided to listen without passing judgment as Bertha explained.

Gretchen was saddened by Bertha's report that she could only remember arriving at that house, a small one-bedroom with a tiny kitchen and living area. Bertha had no recollection of the events leading up to the night she arrived at the house in the marshland. She related that she woke up the next morning feeling very disoriented but was happy to see the sun and to be alive. She came to understand quickly that she was there to care for Ed and Lizzy, an elderly white couple whose adult children lived out of state. Bertha gave the best care to Ed and Lizzy. Before long, they were like a family, with the elders being totally dependent on her. They always looked forward to her reading verses from the Bible before tucking them into bed at night.

Gretchen felt like she was listening to the voice of God as Bertha read, "The kingdom of heaven is like unto a merchant man, seeking goodly pearls. When he had found one pearl of great price, he went and sold all that he had and bought it."[9]

Gretchen listened attentively as Bertha explained that she had been praying for deliverance and believed that the Creator would send a precious pearl. She believed it was Gretchen, the one who had attained gemlike qualities through grueling attrition. She was the one the Creator was preparing to gather His wheat, the one who possessed the spirit of discernment and tolerance, the one who had become a great healer, whose virtues had been constantly under fire.

Gretchen listened as Bertha revealed that she was in college with her in 1994, studying to be a nurse. She related that the parody Gretchen had written and performed on stage about Frederick Douglass was still in her memory. It was then that she realized something special about Gretchen. Bertha also remarked that the Creator knew she would need some backup, having to juggle three jobs and being treated unfairly while raising three children.

"Take courage, Gretchen, for the Creator's unconditional love in you shall overcome all evil."

Gretchen was overtaken by tears and utter joy as she listened to Bertha's soft, sweet voice. She hugged her, and they wept together, giving thanks.

"So, it was you and not Phillis who woke me up to finish my paper the morning it was due, so it wasn't submitted late."

Gretchen was amazed and excited at the same time and continued to question Bertha.

"Was that you who would wake me up every morning at four o'clock and plead with me to write?"

Gretchen needed to know, but she was awakened before Bertha could answer. It was four o'clock in the morning on August 26, 2005, when she started journaling again and promised that she would finish the story.

---

[9] Matthew 13:45–46.

As Gretchen sobbed, Theo handed her a napkin from the table and comforted her. He felt close to her and Bertha now. He continued to listen as Gretchen related further.

She believed that Bertha, the brilliant one, came into existence as a viable spiritual extension of Phillis, a woman who had lived 265 years ago. Gretchen had developed an undying passion to redeem her from a pauper's grave. She was the first African American poet and was born in the 1700s. She was the progenitor who had paved the way for many but had been mistreated. *Phillis* was the name the little girl had to share with the ship in whose bosom she had traveled from West Africa to America. In 1761, she landed in Boston Harbor, Massachusetts, where she was sold into slavery at a tender age of seven. She was given the name "Phillis Wheatley" by a rich merchant whose wife needed a handmaid. Phillis lived with the Wheatley family and grew up to be the most caring, loyal handmaid ever. She had other skills that were exploited but not rewarded. She died in 1784 at thirty-one. It was very painful for Gretchen to even imagine what life might have been for Phillis.

Gretchen affirmed that what the Creator knew, He did predestine.[10] Yet little did she know that she would suffer gross cruelty with no real base of support. She had developed a great passion to write, as the alter ego in her became more fascinated by the similarities in both their lives. Yet due to the lack of historical data and the gap in time and space, the extent of Phillis's sufferings could not be verified. So she had decided to put the thought aside. Although Gretchen had found enough to convince her that Phillis was mistreated, until she met Bertha, there was no way to validate what she thought she knew.

The task on her hands was to interweave the documented

---

[10] Romans 8:29.

evidence and what would be channeled through Bertha in the dream world. Gretchen was unaware until the events began unfolding that her life experiences would be used by the Creator to affirm some of the details.

Gretchen was thirty-seven years old in 1994, when she first heard about Phillis. She learned about her in the American literature course she took in college. While writing a paper about Phillis, Gretchen realized how much they had in common: mind, body, and soul, despite the limited literature about her. She was glad that no mention was made of Phillis's childhood because it would have been too painful for her to read. Gretchen had found various versions of the one portrait done of Phillis with a quill in her hand, at maybe age twelve or thirteen. She sat like an astute thinker and wore a white bonnet and apron, affirming that she was a gentry. Every time Gretchen looked at Phillis's portrait, she would see Bertha, and since 2005, her memory was constantly in her mind.

In April 2011, when Gretchen was experiencing severe financial hardship and on the verge of losing her home to foreclosure, she dreamt about Bertha. Gretchen found out that Ed and Lizzy had passed away. Lizzy died first, in January 2007, and Ed followed six months later, in July. Bertha was brought to Vanityville, Gentry Cove, where she worked for various people. She would walk to the Vanityville Performing Arts Center every Sunday during her half-day off to watch performances. Gretchen followed along in her dream as Bertha related about one Sunday, April 24, 2011. She was given a white handkerchief with a gold letter C embroidered in one corner. It was a gift that came from a young woman who claimed to be her thirty-eight-year-old daughter and whose son, Bertha's grandson, was born in 1994. Bertha told Gretchen that the gesture made her so happy, that someone would consider her a mother and grandmother. She literally passed out. It felt like a dream, although she carried around the handkerchief as proof. Bertha told her that she would go the center every weekend, hoping to meet the young woman again, but it hadn't happened yet.

"It seems a distorted illusion, but I won't give up until the pieces have been put together and validated. Until then, I'll be thankful and faithful," Gretchen told Theo.

"You have my support," he said. "It's no illusion. My beloved wife, Heather, who is now in heaven, also came from West Africa. She wasn't happy about the little she knew about her background, and she didn't have a last name before we got married. Gretchen, all you've related makes sense to me."

She heard his remark and was reassured but wondered who this soul really was. Theo could follow her drift and tried to help her stay focused.

"Please, Gretchen, tell me more. When was the next time you saw Bertha?"

Gretchen tried to remember and then explained that she seemed to have lost track of Bertha until August 25, 2013, when she bumped into her again in a dream. She was attending a health and wellness symposium at Dreamersville Hotel. Gretchen recalled seeing someone sitting in the lobby, reading a book. At first, she wasn't sure it was Bertha, but the curly Afro and radiant smile were convincing. Gretchen noticed also that the name *BERTHA* was printed in white on the back of her fuchsia T-shirt. As Gretchen walked toward her, Bertha got up and met her halfway. Gretchen could see the words "Resurrected Gentry" printed in white on the front of her T-shirt. They hugged each other and held hands.

"Bertha, I am so happy to see you again. How have you been?"

"I'm very happy to see you too, Gretchen. How are you?"

Gretchen could hear her heart beating fast and heeded the urge to respond.

"I'm not truly happy about the events in my life, but I felt a spiritual connection with you that has kept me hopeful."

"I am so sorry," said Bertha as she gestured to Gretchen to sit with her. No sooner had they sat than Gretchen began pouring out what was in her heart.

"I tend to feel doubtful when I try to connect, but you seemed to be reachable only in my dreams."

"When you can't see, you must trust the Creator's lead."

Gretchen was reassured by Bertha's words. She admitted that Bertha's counsel had always been her source of strength and encouragement. When asked where she worked and lived, Bertha's responses were surprising but reassuring. She reported that she had been receiving free room and meals at the Dreamersville Hotel, in exchange for writing ballads, until February 2010. She was happy, although sometimes she'd gone without food for days and had to sleep in a shelter.

Gretchen was very sorry to hear this and wished her situation were different so she could help Bertha. She could truly identify with Bertha's struggles, which were the same sort of oppression she was feeling. Bertha's response to Gretchen's question of how she coped when she wasn't writing was ironic. Bertha related that she would go to the arts center in Vanityville, unnoticed, until she was made to start wearing her ID T-shirt in 2011. She always enjoyed listening to her own poetry being read by others. Yet sometimes she wished for the opportunity to perform on stage. That was when Gretchen got the idea for the title of her book, *Resurrected Gentry Crossing Over*. She shared with Bertha that she dreamed to see her soar above the cruel realm to a safer, more peaceful place. She longed to see *Resurrected Gentry Crossing Over*, the great divide in her angelic flight to home. Gretchen believed that Bertha was created to be the angel of light, to lead the downtrodden home.

"You are amazing, and I hope someday to follow in your footsteps," Gretchen heard Bertha say and tried to convince her otherwise.

"I am the one following in your footsteps. You are the child prodigy, the genius writer-poet who has been robbed of your rightful legacy here, as manifested in my dream."

"I could never walk a mile in your shoes, Dr. Gretchen Mocktruman, my Li'l Pearl."

Gretchen felt contented by Bertha's words but insisted on being the facilitator who would redeem Bertha/Phillis from a pauper's grave.

"Gretchen, you are a philosopher, healer, and humanitarian; I could never be that," Bertha said, in awe of Gretchen's legacy.

Gretchen continued to believe that Phillis, through Bertha, had paved the way for her success and given her the will to persevere. They deserved recognition beyond a pauper's grave. This was their story that the Creator had ordered Gretchen to write. In response to their passionate cry for help, the Creator had begun a good work in them, and they would be faithful to complete it.[11] Yet again, Gretchen heard Bertha's captivating words: "This I know is certain: I shall decrease for you to increase."

In that precise moment, Gretchen realized for the first time that Bertha needed for her to heed her voice.

When you can't see, you must trust the Creator's lead.

Then Gretchen could see that the words printed on the back of Bertha's T-shirt had changed. She noticed that the word *BERTHA* was replaced by an angel dressed in purple with white wings, soaring above the words *Crossing Over*. The front still had the words "Resurrected Gentry" printed on it. Gretchen could hear their hearts beating as one amid the silence as they embraced each other and cried tears of joy.

They wiped each other's tears away. Then Bertha gently tugged on Gretchen's hand and led her to the brown sectional sofa in the lobby, where they sat and continued chatting. She knew that Gretchen understood but still needed guidance.

"What do those words mean to you?" Gretchen asked, curious to know.

---

[11] Philippians 1:6.

Ascension of the Creator's faithful servant, crossing the deadly divide...

Gretchen was convinced that they were both passionate about praising the Creator and fulfilling His plan for their redemption. She listened as Bertha reported that she wore the three T-shirts— fuchsia, teal, and blue—with the words "Resurrected Gentry" printed on them, for almost eight years. Yet no one except her and Gretchen cared about the significance of the words. The purpose they served—to be used as a form of identification—was all that mattered to keep the unauthorized out of the center. Gretchen was speechless as she continued to admire Bertha's brilliance and wisdom that had earned her a free pass to enjoy her poetry. She couldn't help noticing Bertha's athletic look in blue denim pants and black ballet flats. Her complexion was radiant, and her smile was beautiful.

"How could the world not recognize you, Bertha? Your presence exudes light and makes the heart glow. It gives a feeling of hope to the hopeless."

"My soul knows very well that I am wonderfully made to be used by the Creator according to His good works."[12]

Gretchen also understood that the Creator would make a way, but she was curious to know how Bertha got around, since like her, she didn't drive and did not have any family support. She was glad to know that Bertha had a reliable bus service, and while she liked being alone, it bothered her a bit to be considered insignificant, no more than a foreigner in Gentry Cove. A few of her clients had openly refused her care. No matter how good we get, we will never be good enough for everyone.

In a positive light, she said, "We are called to be excellent at what is good, and we should never give up." These words were reassuring to them both.

Gretchen shared Bertha's belief that suffering may intensify as

---

12 Psalm 139:14.

it is designed to make us feel unloved, discouraged, destabilized, and hopeless. She agreed with Mother Theresa that being unwanted, unloved, had a worse effect on the human soul than hunger or poverty. They'd always wanted to do more, to help care for others. They were very thankful for the education they'd received, and their desire was to utilize what they'd learned in making a difference, to serve humanity more.

Another thing that stood out in Gretchen's recall was when Bertha pointed to the title of the article in her hand: "Injustice, Suffering, Difference: How Can Community Health Nursing Address the Suffering of Others?"

Bertha explained that the article was critical of the inconsistencies in social justice. It argued that being disconnected from others makes suffering normal, which was a form of social injustice. The article supported the argument that collectively, we should all feel responsible for the well-being of each other, despite cultural differences. We must avoid indifference toward others.

Gretchen felt that social injustice was a serious concern that adversely impacted and devastated thousands of lives, including hers and Bertha's (and Phillis's, for that matter). Americans who dedicated their lives in excellent service had been mistreated and rejected because of social and cultural differences.

Gretchen agreed that more should be done to enhance social awareness. They needed to strengthen the voices that spoke out against human suffering and wickedness in high places.[13] There was a critical need for social reform against injustice. She wholeheartedly supported Bertha's belief that the Creator had heard their cry and would keep that which they'd committed unto Him against that day.[14]

"Bertha also knew how much I enjoyed being in her company. We embraced, chatted some more, and attended a music festival

---

[13] Ephesians 6:12–13.

[14] 2 Timothy 1:12.

later that evening and then had dinner," Gretchen recalled. "It was the last time I saw her."

———◇———

A moment's silence elapsed as Gretchen and Theo watched the waitress set down another round of margarita mocktails. Theo graciously thanked the waitress and Gretchen for the hospitality. He sipped his margarita as the waitress stepped away and noticed that Gretchen was silent and looked sad. In trying to reassure her, he discovered that she regretted not keeping connected with Bertha. She recalled that the news reporter had mentioned that Bertha worked for Skip's employment agency the day before her accident. She was never happy working for him and often complained about being overworked and underpaid. She had related that it was a very painful and devastating experience when she was laid off from work for three years.

"Why did she go back into such a terrible situation?" Theo asked.

"Well, a logical reason could be because that's Bertha. She's like me: very forgiving and loyal, or it might have simply been about survival. She had bills to pay. Unfortunately, victims are often blamed and made to feel guilty that they've contributed to their abuse."

"I do agree. However, Bertha was capable of better. She is a very qualified, talented, and hardworking person."

"We were all that and more until we became marginalized, downtrodden, and powerless."

"Did that happen to you too, Gretchen?"

"Yes, but let's stay in Bertha's corner for the time being. In her defense, I know her well enough to believe that she was putting love for service above self. It made her oppressor work even harder to destroy all her strength, to ultimately kill her joy. Isn't that what evil would do?"

"Yes, that's what evil would do. People who are inclined to be unfair will also take advantage of the less fortunate and be merciless."

"You've just described Skip exactly. I totally agree."

"I am very sorry for what you and Bertha have gone through, but don't lose hope; you have a right to be here. Justice shall prevail, in due course. We have a mandate to subdue evil, and God is in control."

"Thanks for the encouragement. I shall surely follow your advice, and by His redeeming grace, I shall continue the good works."

Theo noticed the time on his cell phone screen; it was 10:30. He got up to leave and announced, "On Bertha's behalf, thank you, Gretchen. I'm very impressed by your genuine love and concern for Bertha, and I must admit to you that I do feel very attached to her as well."

"Theo, I feel compelled to do this. If you don't mind, I'd like you to join me when I go visit Bertha at the hospital tomorrow."

"I'd be delighted to join you, and I'm sure that'll make Bertha happy too."

"I have an early appointment in Vanityville. What's a good time for us to meet?"

"I'll be available after ten o'clock in the morning," Theo replied, excusing himself for a bathroom break.

Gretchen had time to reflect on her meeting so far with Theo. She thought he was one of the nicest people in the world, and there was no doubt in her mind that he could be trusted. She felt strongly that he was sent by the Creator to support both her and Bertha.

"Sorry for having to end this very important and interesting conversation so abruptly, but I did tell my son that I'd be home by midnight. Plus, I have a very important meeting first thing in the morning. Therefore, I must be going."

"You don't need to explain, I understand," Gretchen said as they shook hands.

"It was a pleasure meeting you, Gretchen, and I'll be calling to confirm the time of our visit with Bertha tomorrow."

"Drive safely and say hello to your family for me. I'll be waiting for your call tomorrow."

Gretchen accompanied Theo into the lobby and watched as he exited the front door of the hotel.

Chapter 3

On Monday, August 14, 2017, Theo told Gretchen that he had resigned his job at the center. He explained that he had been on time for his eight o'clock meeting with Dr. Trent Nun, the headmaster at the Performing Arts Center in Vanityville. As he walked into Trent's office, Theo's eyes were fixed on him as he sat at his desk.

Trent is still looking young, being in his seventies like me, Theo reflected. *Maintaining good health is surely helping.*

Theo greeted Trent, and the moment he sat in the chair across from his desk, he asked, "Can you tell me what's going on? Why am I here on my day off?"

"I should be asking the questions, Dr. Worlington."

Theo watched as Trent showed him the newspaper article and he read the caption: "Performing Arts' Center Psychologist Sought for Questioning: Hero or a Suspect?"

Theo was livid.

"What? I'm confused. Is this a joke? Where did this come from?"

I'm sorry that I have to be the first one to break this news to you," Trent said. "I didn't mean to ambush you. The stranger you rescued has gone missing. Where were you after midnight last night?"

"I was minding my business," Theo replied. "You ought to try it."

Margaret Poole

"Good answer. However, it's not funny when a woman you were last seen visiting winds up missing, and not even your own son could reach you."

"I don't think it's funny when people are trying to make me the criminal, when I'm the one who truly has Bertha's best interest at heart. I rescued her from death. Why would I make her disappear? Furthermore, how could she have disappeared from the intensive care unit?"

"You need to report to law enforcement, if you haven't done so yet. It states here that you are a prime suspect."

Trent read from the article to Theo: "Dr. Worlington is listed as a person of interest and a prime suspect in the disappearance of a woman known only as 'Bertha.' She was evacuated from a wrecked car in Marshvalley Creek. Dr. Worlington was the first to arrive at the scene and called EMS. Bertha was reported to be on life support but stable condition when she disappeared from Vanityville Hospital. Dr. Worlington was reported as the last person to visit her."

"I am so sickened by the whole thing," Theo snapped, "and to think that you of all people would believe that I have anything to do with this."

He noticed the puzzled look on Trent's face as he probed.

"In light of your bizarre behavior recently, including your frequent absences, your involvement is certainly questionable. Where have you been for the past week?"

"If it makes you happy, I spent most of the time with Bertha at the hospital, and last night, I was with her friend."

"Who is this Bertha you keep mentioning, and what is your relationship with her?"

"I'll allow law enforcement to do their investigation and meanwhile resign from my job here, effective today." Theo was obviously upset.

"Don't shoot the messenger," Trent said.

"This is the most horrific time of my life," Theo muttered.

"Indeed, this is a terrible situation for you to be in," Trent said. "Being a nice guy and helping a strange woman is not always a good thing. Would you agree? I also think you should take a sabbatical. A little time away from here would do you some good. Please turn in your keys and whatever material you might have for the center, and I'll send your final paycheck in the mail."

Theo lashed out, feeling annoyed at Trent's accusatory tone.

"You don't get to accuse me and then dictate what I should do. I won't be leaving town. This is where I live. I've done nothing wrong, and the truth will clear my name."

"Theo, please believe me. As the headmaster here, I am only doing my job. Personally, I have nothing against you," Trent remarked as he reached out to Theo for a handshake. "Let me know if I can help in any way," he added.

Theo refused to shake Trent's hand.

"No, thank you. You've helped enough already," Theo snapped as he walked past Trent's outstretched hand and left the office.

No sooner had he walked into the foyer than he was bombarded by a group of news reporters. One reporter was literally in his face, holding a microphone to his mouth. He attempted to walk away, but the reporter was relentless.

"Dr. Worlington, what do you know about Bertha's disappearance?"

"I have nothing to do with Bertha's disappearance. Get out of my face," Theo snapped.

He was accosted by another reporter, who blocked him as he tried to walk away.

"Where were you at ten o'clock last night?"

"Please respect my right to privacy," Theo replied. "I will answer all questions through my attorney. Thank you."

The reporter was still confrontational.

"Were you intimately involved with Bertha?" he asked.

Theo was walking toward his car when he heard Trent's voice

interject: "I think you all should stop harassing Dr. Worlington and leave now. You are trespassing and disturbing the peace here."

Theo slowed his pace to listen, a surprised look on his face.

"He's a prime suspect in a woman's disappearance or death," one of the reporters called out.

Theo had come to a complete halt and turned around to watch the altercation. He saw Trent's tall stature, professional looking, down to his black shoes, confronted the reporters, backing away as they held microphones toward Trent's face.

"I question the veracity in your statement, but I give you the benefit of the doubt," Trent responded in a stern voice. "Now, please leave and allow law enforcement to do their job."

"Thanks, Trent," Theo mumbled to himself, hastening his steps as he resumed his walk toward his Bentley in the parking lot. He watched from inside his car as the reporters dispersed. Then he saw Trent walking very briskly toward his office.

"I'm stunned that Trent reprimanded the reporters on my behalf, but I respect him," said Theo. He sat for a while, thinking to himself. A melancholy feeling came over him, and then he heard someone's laughter coming from the lecture theater, which got him to thinking again.

This Performing Arts Center is surely declining fast, he thought, *although I have some very good memories. I've made the right decision to leave before it gets worse.*

Theo noticed it was 9:20 a.m. on his cell phone, and as he was about to call out, he stopped to answer an incoming call.

"Hey Nate, what's up?"

Theo listened and then responded.

"Yes, I found out this morning after we spoke, and I was confronted about it by the headmaster."

He listened and then responded again.

"I'm very happy that you are starting to understand and to be patient with me. You know me very well. Thanks, son. See you later."

He then made his call, in attempt to connect with Gretchen, but received no response. Deciding not to wait around, he backed out of the parking lot and drove away.

Gretchen had heard her phone vibrate but decided not to take the call because she was in Skip's office, waiting for their meeting to begin. She felt uneasy as he stared at her, but she was dressed appropriately in a black pantsuit, burgundy cowl-neck blouse, and black pumps. She accepted the invitation to have a seat on the guest chair in front of his desk. She noticed that Skip, sitting in a black leather chair, was dressed casually. She was not surprised by the shabby appearance of his office. She could see papers disorganized on his desk, drawers left opened, trash basket full, crumbled papers and files on the floor's dingy carpet.

A couple minutes later, Skip put a caller on speakerphone and spun his chair around, the back facing her as he spoke.

"Hey Trent, I have Gretchen here in my office. She is fully aware of our plan and is ready to get on board with your team."

Gretchen noticed the rattlesnake carved on the back of Skip's chair, and then he turned his chair around to face her again.

"Greetings to you both," Trent said. "I am sorry to be running late for the phone conference with you, Skip. I was delayed due to a crisis here at the center. How are you today, Dr. Mocktruman?"

"Please call me Gretchen. I am well, thanks for asking. How are you?"

"I am well, thank you, and feel free to call me Trent. Sorry about the presentation, and I appreciate your understanding."

"No need to apologize. I am quite aware and believe that things will work out fine."

"I believe they will. Thanks again, Gretchen. As you know, I'd love to hire you as a substitute literature instructor, until a permanent replacement is found. I've decided to trust Skip's recommendation to hire you. He's the chief financial officer on our board of directors and a very important figure in the community."

"I wouldn't recommend her if I didn't think she was capable," Skip said, "and I am only sharing her with you until things calm down here, for me to bring her on board full time. She is eager and available to start right away."

Gretchen listened to the conversation and tried not to appear alarmed at Skip's inappropriate and disrespectful behavior. She noticed that Skip had picked up on her calm demeanor and smiled as Trent continued to speak.

"Gretchen, just to fill you in," Trent said, "we've been in dire need after our previous literature instructor resigned last week. Our organization is indeed falling apart, as she said on her way out. So I truly appreciate your consideration. I must say that I am very impressed by your résumé. You are a very knowledgeable and experienced individual who has worn many hats."

"I know you'll both be happy," Skip said while glancing over at Gretchen, who opted to remain silent.

You've crossed the line to underestimate me, she thought, *but I'll allow your plan to run its course.*

Then she continued to listen in on the telephone conference.

"Skip, I must clear the air about a statement you made in a previous conversation," she heard Trent say.

"I'm listening," said Skip.

"You mentioned that although Gretchen is getting up in age, there will be no regrets; she's good. Do you think her age might be a deterrent?"

"Of course not. This is clearly a misunderstanding. Gretchen's age is not a problem. When do you need her to start?" Skip asked, looking down at the phone as he tried to change focus.

"I would like to meet her this afternoon, if that's okay with you, Gretchen."

"I'll be available at three o'clock," she said.

"That'll be perfect. See you then."

Gretchen took that as a cue to excuse herself.

"Good day, gentlemen," she said as she walked out of Skip's office.

Gretchen could feel Skip's eyes on her and as she exited the door, she heard him raise his voice at Trent.

"How could you do that to me? You should know better."

I believe Trent will be a blessing in disguise, Gretchen told herself.

Then she heard a ding, noticed the word THEO on her cell phone screen, and clicked on the message: "Please call me."

She called Theo and said, "I am so sorry about the delay. I was tied up in a meeting till now."

"Sorry I wasn't there to untie you," he joked.

"Me being tied up is nothing compared ...," Gretchen sounded very upset as she started to reply.

"So you've heard about Bertha's disappearance and that I'm listed as prime suspect," Theo said.

"Yes, and I've already filed a report at the police department that you were with me at the time of her disappearance. I'm sure it is extremely stressful for you, but we must be strong and stay focused. We should concentrate on finding Bertha. There's no need for our trip to the hospital now."

"I agree, and I am very sad, though relieved that I don't have both of you in danger at the same time. Gretchen, I thank you."

"My pleasure. I'll be in touch again later."

That afternoon, Gretchen met with Trent in his office. Her attention was drawn to his prim and proper appearance, looking sharp in his forest green suit with beige shirt, brown tie, and brown shoes. She couldn't help noticing his well-organized office, including a shiny maple bookshelf with encyclopedias and many other books. Trent looked a lot like Theo, except he was a little taller and of lighter complexion, with hazel eyes. Trent made her feel at home, and while they chatted, he invited her to join him in visiting the students in the lecture theater. As they approached the doorway, Gretchen could hear someone yelling.

"That must be our disciplinarian, Nev Axeman," Trent said as he opened the door.

Gretchen could see a very tall, heavyset man with ruddy complexion and curly black hair. He was dressed in a brown suit with white shirt, brown tie, and brown shoes. She listened and watched the reactions as Nev kept scolding.

"I will not tolerate any outrageous behavior at this center," Nev said. "Can somebody tell me what's going on?"

Gretchen noticed that the students were wearing green, short-sleeve polo shirts with the center's red, white, and blue logo and khaki pants or skirts.

"I can, sir, if you promise that I won't be punished for speaking up," a blonde young woman with a British accent said.

"Katandria, we do not punish people for doing the right thing."

Gretchen could see Katandria looking around at her classmates and then heard someone yell out, "You go ahead! Let's hear it!"

Trent tried to distract her attention and escorted her away from the lecture theater, saying, "Come with me, Gretchen. We'll return to the lecture hall later. Clearly, we came at a bad time, but Nev is in control of the situation. He does not take any excuse for unacceptable behavior. I'm sure you'll get to meet him later."

Gretchen nodded and replied, "I quite understand how difficult it must be in your role as headmaster. Keeping everyone happy and motivated for success in such a culturally diverse group of young people must be extremely challenging."

"Thank you for saying that. I am a believer in promoting

diversity. Young people from all walks of life have received training at this center, and there's always room for growth here."

Gretchen believed that Trent was pleased with her demeanor and thought that working with him would be a dream come true. Their conversation gave her a good feeling.

"I have great expectations," she said, "as much as you do, I am sure."

"You bet. I can't wait to see you at work. The students have English literature on Wednesdays and Fridays each week, in seventh period. Although it's on short notice, the syllabus and lesson plans have been completed for you to start lecturing right away. You'll have time earlier in the week to meet other faculty members and get yourself prepared. You have your work cut out for you, but I'll be here for you. When would you be available to start?"

"I can start on this Wednesday, if that's not too soon for you."

"This Wednesday it is."

Two days later, on Wednesday, Gretchen arrived at the lecture hall; Trent was waiting for her. She was looking very professional in a navy-blue skirt suit. Trent greeted the students and introduced her to them.

"I realize that it has been a rough semester for all of us, but we must work together to achieve success," he began. "I also know that you hope to graduate in twenty-four months. You are prepared to work hard, and my staff is ready to work with you. It is my great pleasure to introduce Dr. Gretchen Mocktruman. She is our newest staff member and your literature instructor."

As she stood up and faced the students, Gretchen was greeted with a tepid reception. Yet she felt that her presence on the stage and interesting accent captured everyone's attention.

"Thank you all for the warm introduction and welcome.

I feel privileged to be given the opportunity to take on this huge challenge as your English literature instructor. I am very committed, and I look forward to a rewarding journey with you. I am willing to learn from you, and I hope you will be prepared to learn from me as well. I have great expectations for success, pardon the pun. As we journey together, I'll be the facilitator, helping to bring out the star performers in you all."

Gretchen was stunned by the resounding applause that came next, which ceased as she continued speaking.

"This is our first session, and we are off to a late start, so we'll continue to follow the items outlined in your syllabus. The lectures will be mostly interactive, with a focus on figures of speech and rudiments of English grammar. We'll finish the semester with a play entitled *Trial of the Merchant of Vanityville: The Verdict.* I've been told about your plan to participate in the annual variety show at the Community Center, in about eight weeks. I particularly like the idea of community building, and I believe that your efforts will be memorable."

Gretchen could see a big grin on Trent's face as he nodded and clapped in approval. He gave two thumbs up and quickly left the lecture theater. Gretchen took it as a cue to continue.

She was surprised by everyone's eagerness to participate in the singing and dancing, but only six students signed up to be in the play. The students' primary reason was their reluctance to studying lines, particularly those in Old English.

I have my work cut out for me, she thought, *and I have only eight weeks to make it happen.*

Then to the students, she announced, "Every week, we'll learn ten vocabulary words, starting with the ones today. Your assignment is to look them up, learn their meanings, and use them in a sentence."

She displayed the words on the screen overhead: *metaphor, simile, paradox, oxymoron, personification, hyperbole, irony, pun, alliteration, euphemism.*

Gretchen watched with surprise as the students took snapshots of the words with their cell phones.

Times have certainly changed, she thought to herself, smiling. *Cell phones are the new notebooks.*

Twelve of the twenty-eight students were white, five Hispanics, five African Americans, four Asians, and two Native Americans.

I find it very interesting that half the number of white students, all from European backgrounds, are the only ones willing to participate in the play, Gretchen pondered to herself. Then she continued speaking to the students:

"If you already know some of those words and how they are used in sentences, consider this a refresher course. By the end of eight weeks, you should all be familiar with the first six or seven figures of speech. Everyone's participation in class is very important for success. Are there any questions?"

Gretchen noticed that only one hand went up.

"Go ahead, Katandria," instructed Gretchen, observing the look of surprise on the girl's face as she spoke.

"First of all, Miss Gretchen, if you don't mind telling, how did you know my name?"

"You impressed me with your no-nonsense attitude and distinctive British accent; you've stood out in my mind."

"Thanks, Miss Gretchen. I also need to know the venue for our variety show this year."

"Vanityville Community Center, across from the center's annex.

"Miss Gretchen, I am Annabella, and this is Arsenia. We are happy to have you as our instructor."

Gretchen gave them a smile and thanked the cute Hispanic girl, pointing to the Asian-American sitting to her right.

Gretchen waited a few seconds and then continued, "If no one else has any comments, I'll address this question that some anonymous person left on my desk."

Gretchen read out loud the words on the flashcard she held.

"Dear Miss Gretchen, what do you think about racism?"

She heard the oohs and saw the look of fear on many faces in the lecture theater. She noticed too that others were looking down or had no reaction at all.

"Well, I believe that everyone should be proud of his or her racial or ethnic background, without malice or hatred toward another race; that's racism," Gretchen responded as she displayed the meanings of the word *racism* on the overhead projector for the students to see.

"Words such as intolerance, injustice, prejudice, bias, narrow-mindedness, and discrimination are racially charged. They are linked with other words such as chauvinism, nationalism, xenophobia, and bigotry."

Gretchen was amazed by their reactions when she clicked on each word and they appeared on the screen. The chattering around the hall was not what she had expected on her first day, but it sent a strong message, one she could not ignore. She felt that the impromptu topic of racism had set the stage, and the timing and place were perfect. English literature had evolved over time and was certainly racially charged. So it was difficult to not notice that racism would be a concern and needed to be discussed.

"We can use poetry, prose, drama, and songs as means to express ourselves, using the topic of racism," Gretchen said. "Feel free to say your name and voice your opinion. I have time for five. Then we'll get back on track."

Gretchen could see several hands raised and decided to start with one closest to her on the far right. A tall, slender boy with brown skin and crew-cut hair stood up.

"My name is Malcom. I am seventeen, and I believe that racism is alive but not well among us."

Gretchen couldn't help smiling at the comment, and she heard the laughter around the room as the speaker continued.

"Ignoring it or refusing to talk about it openly, because we don't want to hurt people's feelings, doesn't make racism go away."

Gretchen decided to remain silent while the students applauded for a while.

"Thank you, Malcom," she said, summoning silence as she pointed to a dark-skinned girl in the middle with braided hair.

"Miss Gretchen, I'll be eighteen and will be gone from here soon. My name is Shenee. I am an African American, as you can see, and I agree with Malcom. No one talks about racism around here, until somebody dies because of it. Then they go back to business as usual, after candlelight vigils, prayers, and media frenzy, blaming mental illness, but no real solution for it."

Gretchen noticed that not many students were clapping, but almost all had a sad look on their faces. She pointed to a boy in the back.

"I second that. My name is Hercules, and my parents and I came to America from Greece sixteen years ago. My story is about my Indian friend here, Rami. He is fourteen, our youngest nerd."

Gretchen made eye contact with the frail-looking Indian sitting to the right of Hercules, a muscular youth, olive complexion, and curly, shoulder-length hair.

"Has anyone in this classroom ever reached out to Rami since he's been here, six months now?"

Gretchen noticed the silence and saw the look of surprise on many faces as Hercules continued his story.

"Well, I did, about three weeks ago, when I was traveling home on the bus, and it sunk in for the first time that I was a snob. I would always go to sit beside a white person, but that day, there was no seat, except one in the back where Rami sat. Later that day, Rami sent me a text: 'Hello, my name is Rami and I would like to be your friend.'

"I deleted his text and threatened to beat him up if he ever texted me again. Rami never came back to the center until two weeks later, when his mother was in trouble for him skipping classes. I nearly got expelled when the truth came out, and I thank God that he could forgive me. Rami is my friend, and we ride the bus and hang out all the time."

Gretchen joined in the applause, then her attention was fixed on another student sitting in the back, to her left.

"I hear you, bro. My name is Juan Tapper Pepe, and I am a seventeen-year-old Latino-American. I have seen first-hand how racism has ruined innocent people's lives. When you are teamed up against, lied to, and bullied because you are not from their race, it's excruciating. Racism hurts, bro."

Gretchen was starting to feel at home with the students. She applauded with them and listened along as another student, a tall, handsome lad, spoke.

"I am Patrick, and I turned eighteen last week. I am also proud to be a white guy who has been raised by parents with morals. I will agree that racism is very much a negative force in our society. As the younger generation, we must do whatever we can to bring more awareness and education about overcoming its ill effects. Racism seeks to divide and conquer, but love is greater."

Amid the applause, Gretchen embraced each of the young people who spoke.

"I was touched by your comments about racism. I am sure there are many more, but time does not allow," she remarked.

"Ah, please, Miss Gretchen, one more. My name is Miwa, and I am sixteen years old and Asian-American. I have something to say about racism, and it will take me less than a minute."

Gretchen noticed her resemblance to Arsenia; they both had shoulder-length, straight hair and tanned complexions.

"Okay, Miwa, you have a minute."

"Thank you, Miss Gretchen. I must say that attending this arts center has been the most rewarding time of my life. I've made friends with a diverse group of people, and I've learned to take ownership for my actions. My experiences here have taught me how to overcome my own racial prejudices, and I am trying to teach my parents to do the same."

"Good for you, Miwa," Gretchen said as she joined in the applause and noticed the big smile on Miwa's face.

"I am inspired, and I thank you all. For those of you who did not participate today, there will be other opportunities to share your stories."

Gretchen decided to end the day's session and announced, "Now that we have gotten racism off our chests, in closing, please note that we'll have a rehearsal every Friday for the next three weeks leading up to our big night. If there are no questions, you are dismissed. Be safe and treat each other with kindness and respect.

At the end of that Friday's session, Gretchen responded to a text to meet with Trent in his office. She sat across from him, listening as he explained that someone had taped the session, and a few parents were concerned that racism was being taught instead of English literature.

Gretchen was silent for a few seconds after Trent stopped the tape.

"I was speechless when I heard this," he began. "I know you have good intentions, so please, don't allow this little incident to deter you. I only need for you to be careful what you do and say."

"I have nothing to say at the moment," she replied, "but I promise to address this soon."

Chapter 4

Later that day, as Gretchen was exiting the Vanityville Community Center's gift shop, she noticed a young man approaching. She quickly stepped out of the way to avoid a collision.

"Oops! Sorry, ma'am," he said.

Gretchen watched as he put away his cell phone and held the door for her to step out first.

"Thank you. Nateandro Worlington?" Gretchen asked.

She could see little resemblance to Theo in the tall, handsome young man staring back at her with his greenish-brown-hazel eyes. He had curly short hair and a brown complexion, and he was wearing a forest-green polo shirt, blue jeans, and brown loafers.

"Yes, ma'am. I apologize for bumping into you like that. Ah, I don't recall having met you before."

"I don't think so, but I've seen pictures of you, and I happen to have met your dad."

"Oh, and who do I have the pleasure of meeting?"

"Dr. Gretchen Mocktruman," she said as she shook Nate's outstretched hand.

"Nice to meet you, Dr. Mocktruman. So, you must be the new English lit instructor. Dad did mention you."

"Nice to meet you, Nate. Please call me Gretchen."

"Welcome to Vanityville, Miss Gretchen. Is this your first time here?"

"Well, I've visited Vanityville over the past four years; my friend Bertha lived in Dunkersfield. We would come down here to the arts festivals. She was a poetry enthusiast."

Gretchen noticed that Nate was staring at her as if he'd seen a ghost.

"I hope you'll like it here," he said, trying to ignore the subject of Bertha, which Gretchen figured had made him a bit uneasy.

"Yes, I hope so too. I must be going, but we'll meet again, I'm sure."

"I'll definitely let my dad know that we've met."

Gretchen heard Nate's remark but was more focused on his reaction when she mentioned Bertha. She started to feel that her time in Vanityville would be very interesting. Her attention was drawn to the statue of a male athlete, his stalwart expression carved regally in stone, near the entrance to the community center. She stopped briefly to study his face—the strong jawline, the pouty lips, the confidence in his stance—and recognized it as Nate's.

An impressive-looking statue of a football player and role model, she thought. *Meeting the Worlington family is like a dream come true.*

That Sunday, Gretchen was again coming out of the Community Center's gift shop when she saw Nate standing in line at the cashier's stand, talking to a young lady. She decided to wait until he was done, when the headline on the front page of the *Vanityville Tabloid* caught her attention. "Bertha: The Missing Stranger." Gretchen walked over to the magazine rack, picked up a copy, and went toward the cashier stand. Her attention shifted to a blurred picture of Bertha in the hospital bed.

"Well, look who I've bumped into again. The lovely Miss Gretchen! How are you today?" she heard Nate ask as her gaze shifted from the magazine in her hand to him.

"Hi, Nate. Good to see you again. This is a small town, indeed."

"Indeed. Please meet Meemee, my fiancée."

"Hello, Miss Gretchen, nice to meet you. I've heard many wonderful things about you."

"Nice to meet you too, Meemee, and I'm sure we'll be talking about many wonderful things."

Meemee gave her a hug and told her how pretty she looked.

"Thank you, Meemee. You are so adorable."

Gretchen thought Nate and Meemee were a loving couple. She found Meemee to be very attractive; she looked like the singer Nancy Wilson. Meemee was a little shorter than Nate, and her tropical-floral chiffon minidress complimented his tangerine shirt and tan shorts.

The three were leaving the gift shop when Gretchen tried calling Leo, her private driver, but was unable to connect with him.

"I'd be honored to drive you home," she heard Nate offer and realized it was going to be difficult to say no.

"I'd be happy to learn more about you too," Meemee interjected.

"Thanks for the offer, but you don't have to go out of your way."

Gretchen tried to decline but lost to Nate and Meemee when she heard a clap of thunder, noticed the dark clouds overhead, and felt raindrops.

"Okay. I sense a thunderstorm coming, and I can't get a hold of Leo, so I'll ride with you. Thanks."

Nate quickly opened the car door for her.

"There's lots of room in this car," he said, "and you don't need to risk getting drenched while you wait for your ride."

Gretchen noticed that Nate and Meemee were genuinely pleased with her company. She looked on with great admiration at the young couple and listened attentively from her seat in the rear, behind Meemee.

Nate started the engine and asked, "Where are we going, Miss Gretchen?"

"I'm sorry. My address is 504 Sandknoll Circle in South Cove Estates, about fifteen minutes north of here."

"Don't be sorry, I'll take you anywhere. Besides, I also live in South Cove Estates," he said.

"Small town," they said in unison.

"Buckle up, kiddos," he said as he put the car in gear and pushed the gas.

Gretchen could tell how proud Nate was of his car. It was rather nice. She'd never been in a Porsche before. It wasn't quite as roomy in the backseat as she might hope, but the car sure did go fast. Once they were on the road, Gretchen started probing.

"If you don't mind me asking, Nate, where did you get your charming personality?"

"I would say from both my parents. A little from each, and a lot I've cultivated as I grew up. My mom was very creative and had a keen sense of humor."

"She must be very proud of you," Gretchen interjected.

"I'm not sure if Dad told you, but Mom succumbed to breast cancer when I was seventeen years old, thirteen years ago."

"Your dad did share a little about her. I'm very sorry. Didn't mean to upset you."

"That's okay, ma'am. I have grown to accept my loss. Moreover, Meemee and her family have become a remarkable source of support for Dad and me. We've known them for seven years.

"He is my heartthrob and best friend," said Meemee.

"She was my high school sweetheart, and through our ups and downs, while in university, I've grown even more attached to her, particularly this past year."

"Nate and I are soul mates," Meemee concurred.

"As for Dad, Theodorus Worlington, he is my rock, next to God. He is a fun-loving, extremely caring and loyal person, the brains in the family. He will never stop loving Mom and me. It was difficult to watch him go through grief when Mom died.

Despite our differences and my feeling neglected at times, Dad is a very strong support system for me. He is also very protective over at-risk youths and people who can't fend for themselves. I will never understand how he could be labelled a suspect in that woman's disappearance."

"I can relate to your apparent distress; thank you for verbalizing your feelings. I believe that your dad didn't mean to neglect you. Sometimes, we get so caught up in the moment, caring for others, that we lose sight of our family's needs."

"It bothered me a bit to think that he would be so into a total stranger, in an unconscious state of mind, and cannot even hear me speak. I worry for his mental health."

"I believe that you both love each other dearly, but sometimes, a situation requires that you put the needs of others first. Maybe his sensitivity to Bertha's critical condition clashed with your need for his affection?"

Gretchen tried to agree with Nate while putting Theo's action in her own perspective.

"I guess that might be reasonable to say. I also believe that Dad's a very lonely man, needing affection I can't give him."

Gretchen could see Nate looking at her through his rearview mirror as he remarked, "I think Dad will be fine, and your company means a lot to him."

"Thank you for sharing those sentiments about your dad. I believe this is a very sad moment for all of us, and I'm glad we have each other."

As Nate's car approached the north end of Marshvalley Creek bridge, Gretchen heard the roar of an engine behind them and the screeching of tires. She watched as Nate veered his car to the right, went off the road, and came to a screeching halt alongside the boardwalk. He turned on his hazard lights after putting the car in park.

Gretchen was in a bit of a shock but heard Nate ask if everyone was okay. There was no response from Meemee, who slowly got the words out that she was okay. Then Gretchen, after taking a couple deep breaths, said that she was okay too. She could see Nate looking to his right at Meemee; he reached over and gently rubbed her shoulder. Gretchen could see Nate looking at her and asked again if she was okay. She thanked him for his alertness, quick reaction time, and caring attitude.

"I could see from my rearview mirror that a red pickup truck was tailgating me; he deliberately tried to run us off the road and into the creek. I would have chased him down if you ladies weren't in the car."

"I am very happy that no one got hurt, though I'm shaken up a bit," said Gretchen.

"Honey, do you know anyone who would want to run us over?" Meemee asked, looking over at Nate while she massaged his shoulder in return.

"I have no idea," he said.

"Someone was definitely trying to send a strong message, and it must be reported to law enforcement. I only caught a piece of the license plate, but I took a snapshot of the bridge as well," Gretchen remarked.

She noticed that the thunderstorm had ceased, but the visibility was still poor. Nate cautiously turned onto Coventry Landing and then turned onto South Cove Estate Drive. Shortly after, Nate's car pulled up into Gretchen's driveway. The couple accompanied her into her house. She embraced them and thanked Nate as he promised to file a report with Vanityville Police Department.

Chapter 5

It was Sunday afternoon, one week after Bertha's accident and subsequent disappearance. Gretchen had journaled about her first week at the center. Afterward, she was feeling very bored and a bit depressed, being alone in her one-bedroom apartment. So she decided to take a leisurely ride to the community park.

Gretchen sat on a bench near the pond in the park and enjoyed the warm atmosphere around her. She was feeling uplifted and relaxed. She noticed a brown duck with her brood of about eight ducklings gliding in the pond. She heard the mother duck quacking, as if telling her little ones to stay in line. Gretchen was one with nature, and it was the best feeling ever. She enjoyed looking at the green, gold, and red maples, oaks, sycamore, and pine trees, and the lush green grass on the park ground.

Breathtaking, she thought.

Then she decided to listen to the microcassette tape she'd found. She retrieved the tape and recorder from her purse. She scrutinized the tape and then inserted it into the tape recorder. She was surprised to recognize the voices on the tape.

"Skip, I know you told me that you are holding no grudges, but I'm not so sure about that. You mentioned feeling optimistic that she would do well as a substitute teacher. Yet you didn't seem to support the idea that she should be the be master of ceremonies at our variety show."

"Listen, Trent, if I were you, I would not allow Gretchen to have a high-profile role. I don't think she should be given such a huge role because of cultural differences. But at the end of the day, it's your call. I can't tell you what to do."

"I agree that you can't tell me what to do, but in this situation, things are a little different. I must get a thorough background check on her, to clear the air. Otherwise, I feel good about her abilities. She'd be an excellent asset for any organization."

"Trent, as you know, a few dignitaries will be attending the variety show. Plus, I'll have to answer to members of the board. I don't want to be embarrassed there."

"Well, I know too that Gretchen is a naturalized US citizen, with First Amendment rights. I'll fill you in on the details later. Let's concentrate on her work for now and make sure she does a good job."

Gretchen clicked off the tape and sat there for a moment, thinking, with a look of disgust on her face.

"Something is definitely wrong here," she said aloud, "but I'll go with my heart for now. No time to throw a pity party. I have work to do; the students are depending on me."

Gretchen heard a horn toot and knew it was Leo, returning to drive her home. She was very grateful for her new driver. Leo was very dependable and good-natured; he always made her feel blessed. He was always on time. The only challenge she had was the language barrier. He spoke very little English, and Gretchen's goal was to brush up on her Spanish.

On arriving home, Gretchen was feeling more energized and decided to do laundry and prepare herself for work. She was adjusting slowly to her new one-bedroom apartment, compliments of Skip. She has been trying to come to terms with the sad memories, which got worse when she was home.

The next morning, Gretchen felt confident after she prayed about speaking to Skip. As they drove in silence in his black Lexus, she thought about speaking to him another time, but her heart had told her differently. She noticed that he glanced across at her once or twice, and the grim look on his face did make her feel uneasy. It was difficult for her to muster the courage to initiate a conversation. Eventually, after they drove in silence for about five minutes, she thanked Skip for all the good things he had done for her: the apartment, the job, the rides.

"Due diligence," he said.

"Deadly deception—the plan to get rid of me," Gretchen replied, feeling unafraid.

"No time for small talk. Are you happy in your job?"

"The truth is, I'm always happy in my job, putting service before self, and you know that's not small talk."

"Trent is happy with you. He thinks you're a great asset for the center."

"Well, then, I am happy for him too, thank you."

"Good. I knew you would be," Skip said.

The car swerved right at South Cove Estates Drive onto Coventry Landing. She noticed, for the first time, "Coventry Landing" written on a mound of grass, with purple cornflowers around the base. A few seconds later, the car went across Coventry Landing Boulevard and right onto Marshvalley Creek bridge/Gentry Cove Highway. To her surprise, Skip blamed her for causing him to nearly miss his turn and called her a poor navigator.

"Sorry," she said as she kept her gaze ahead on the twisted rail at the foot of the bridge. She recalled the red pickup truck overtaking Nate's car and nearly causing it to crash with her, Nate, and Meemee in it. As Skip's Lexus headed south toward the center, Gretchen noticed that he was watching her closely.

"I'll try to pay attention," she explained, "so you won't miss another turn."

"That's okay. When I made that sharp right turn at the fork,

I had it in mind to go straight across to North Cove Estate, where I live."

"Oh, I see," Gretchen replied. "While there is time, can you tell me why I was transferred to the center, instead of working at your wellness center?"

"We can have that discussion another time. At least you like the job, and that's all we should care about at the moment."

"I realize what's important to you, but I am unhappy being kept in the dark. I feel like I'm being manipulated."

"Get to the point," he snapped. "Who is manipulating you?"

After a brief pause, Gretchen tried to explain to Skip why she believed that what had happened to Bertha might happen to her. To her surprise, Skip changed the subject; he didn't want to talk about Bertha. She didn't believe she had anything to lose, so she continued speaking.

"Bertha was constantly exploited," she said, "because of her love and dedication to be of service to humanity."

"I have no idea what you are rambling about," Skip said.

"She is a dear friend of mine who disappeared while in hospital."

Gretchen noticed that there was no reaction from Skip, so she continued to speak.

"It's been all over the news for over a week now, and Vanityville is a small town. Haven't you heard?"

"Oh, that news. I don't know her, so that's why I couldn't remember."

"I know that she worked for you up to Friday, the day before she nearly died in a car crash."

Gretchen felt like she was gaining ground with Skip. She informed him that she didn't feel comfortable participating in the upcoming variety show.

"Well, I'd rather not discuss other people's personal affairs with you, but she was an independent contractor. Now take my advice: leave detective work to the experts."

Gretchen listened carefully and decided she should put more focus on teaching at the center for the time being.

"Consider yourself lucky to be living in my neighborhood, at my expense. I'll let it go this time, if you can pretend that we didn't have this conversation."

Gretchen felt humiliated, but she also understood the reason behind it. She grew calmer as she remembered the inspiring words: *Be not afraid or dismayed, the battle belongs to the Lord.*

"I'm trying to communicate with you. Why are you so uptight and self-righteous? What does your Christianity teach you?" Skip asked.

It was confirmation to Gretchen that a spiritual warfare existed between them, and she decided not to respond.

Seconds later, she felt the car skid as Skip slowed down. She concluded that he seemed agitated, as usual. His behavior made her even more suspicious.

He pulled up to the curb near the walkway leading to the center's main building.

Before getting out of the car, Gretchen said, "Thanks again, and moving forward, I'd appreciate some validation. Hope to see you at the upcoming variety show."

She noticed that Skip did not respond. The black Lexus sped off as soon as she closed the door. As she walked toward the center, she told herself to be patient and allow the story to unfold.

Later that afternoon, Gretchen made another attempt to connect with Theo but got his voicemail.

She realized for the first time that her heart yearned for Theo's company. When she met up with him that night at his home, he told her about his visit to Skip's office.

Theo recalled that he was sitting in the waiting area of Skip's office and overheard a conversation:

"Butch, I'm telling you to back off. I demand an explanation. Why did you leave me out of the plan, and what does Berba have to do with it?"

Theo noticed that the receptionist had stepped away, so he moved to the closest chair, a few feet from the office door. He could hear clearly as the talking got louder.

"Skip, please keep your voice down and listen to me. I can assure you that Colanda's insurance money will be put to good use. Who cares what Berba's role is?"

"I care, and I don't want him involved in anything that concerns me. He is a loser and has no morals."

"I agree, but you're not a good example of morality yourself."

"I don't have blood on my hands."

"What are you implying?"

"It's not an implication. It is a statement of fact, and you know what I'm talking about."

"And what else do I know, illegitimate one?"

"Butch, I get the point. You have one on me."

"I think you should stop worrying about me and keep an eye on them two lovebirds while I concentrate on what to do about Bertha. I need to find her."

"I'll keep both eyes on them. I give Gretchen a ride almost every day. She's starting to speak out and knows a lot more than I thought."

Theo moved away from the door before it opened, and Butch walked out. Gretchen followed along in her mind as Theo described a bald-headed white man, clean-shaven, tall, medium build, with a paunch. He was dressed like a cowboy, in blue jeans with a plaid shirt and leather boots. Theo thought it strange that he was dressed like a cowboy.

"Hey, Theo," Butch said. "What brings you this way?"

"I needed to speak with you."

"What about?"

"As you know, I'm Nate's father. I saw you delivering a package at my house about a month ago. What's up with that?"

"I thought he would have told you; I was trying to connect him with a job in a sports medicine company."

"Well, don't contact him anymore. He doesn't need a job from you. Stay away from my family, okay? Next time, I won't be talking to you."

"Your son is a grown man and can speak for himself. Besides, I can do whatever I want. Don't you dare threaten me!" Butch retorted as he walked away.

Theo and Gretchen sat on the sofa in his living room. She took the time to update him about her suspicion that Trent was not aware of Skip's real personality. Gretchen agreed with Theo that Skip and Butch, and others including Berba, might know about Bertha's disappearance. Gretchen was also concerned that Colanda's safety might be at risk. She appreciated that Theo was impressed by her courage and ability to cope with all the stressful situations around her, while grieving over Bertha's disappearance.

"Gretchen, it's tearing me up inside to know that you are affected by this dreadful situation. I'm hoping that it won't be for too long."

"Thank you, Theo. I feel the same way too."

"From now on, I'll drive you to work, and if I can't, I'll arrange your ride; is that okay?"

"I appreciate your wanting to protect me, but I am concerned about your safety and Nate's as well."

Theo looked into her eyes and kissed her on the forehead.

"I really believe we are going to be victorious," he said. "I have a hunch that Skip and his cohorts were involved in the attempt to take Nate's life. I won't say anything further now, but you must be careful. Promise?"

"I promise," said Gretchen.

Chapter 6

Two days later, on Wednesday afternoon, Gretchen felt blended in with the students at the center, who wore gold polo shirts, the color of the day. She had no doubt that she stood out as the invigilator in her gold blouse, brown pantsuit, and tan pumps. She felt pleased as she watched all twenty-eight students quietly take their first quiz. She could see how focused they were and believed that everyone was determined to do well. Yet Gretchen couldn't help noticing the two dozen empty seats in the back.

There is much room and potential for growth in this place, she thought. *I thank the Creator for sending me here.*

Gretchen realized that she had been working at the center as if she were a full-time instructor. She spent a great portion of her time accomplishing a few routine duties and took on some additional tasks. She was constantly busy reviewing lesson plans, preparing for activities, grading papers, attending faculty meetings, following up with concerned parents, and preparing for the variety show. She stayed up until the wee hours of the night, sometimes getting only a few hours of sleep. Yet she felt content, knowing that her students were happy, and she was getting the job done.

At the end of the session, Gretchen collected the twenty-eight test papers. Then she gathered her belongings and left the lecture hall.

———◇———

Friday afternoon, Gretchen was the busiest she'd ever been. At the end of the class session, she decided to review the list of participants for the upcoming show. She had noticed that only six names were submitted for the play, and only one for the piano solo; everyone wanted to either dance or sing. Then she began entering the quiz grades in the computer, while she waited for Nate to pick her up. She remained in the lecture hall and texted herself some inspired ideas for her journal. She was so engrossed in her thoughts that it took a text message from Nate to alert her that he was waiting in the parking lot.

Later, as she stepped out of his Porsche into Theo's driveway, she was forced to put thoughts of the center and everything else aside. Gretchen's attention was drawn to Nate as he helped Meemee from the car. They were both wearing jeans and red shirts with long-sleeves. Gretchen felt more comfortable in her striped, long-sleeve blouse and jeans after Meemee told her how chic she looked.

Then Gretchen's attention shifted to a two-story, yellow brick house across the street with beautiful flowers lining both sides of the driveway. She was surprised to see Miwa, her Asian-American student who was working on how to overcome her own racial prejudices while trying to teach her parents.

Miwa's mother, dressed in floral shirt and white slacks, was tugging on Miwa's hand as she was trying to wave. Miwa was in Friday's uniform of the day: a lavender polo shirt and khaki skirt. Gretchen looked back just in time to see Miwa and her mom staring at her.

Then Gretchen's attention was shifted back to Nate and Meemee as she walked behind them toward the front door of the Worlingtons' house.

She heard Nate call out as they entered Theo's family room, "Hey, Dad, we're here."

Gretchen could feel her heart beating fast when she saw Theo; she sensed that he was happy to see her too.

"Hello, Nate," Theo said. "I was just tidying up the kitchen."

Gretchen saw the surprised look on Theo's face when she entered the living room and as Nate jumped ahead of her, she heard Theo say, "You all look so patriotic in those colors."

"And you, so complimentary in white and navy-blue sweater and navy pants," said Meemee.

"I had planned to go jogging but changed my mind because I would've missed this occasion," Theo explained and smiled at Gretchen.

"Dad, I should have mentioned that Gretchen would be attending your birthday party," Nate said, "but I decided to surprise you."

"That's perfectly fine, son. Gretchen is welcomed here anytime."

Gretchen was very pleased to hear this.

Theo gave Nate and Meemee a hug. Then he walked over to Gretchen with open arms, and she walked toward him. They held hands, and he spoke to her in a soft tone.

"Nice to see you again, Gretchen. You look lovely, as usual."

She could feel a calmness she'd never felt before.

"Meemee, let's get ready for the party," Nate suggested.

Theo smiled and nodded in agreement.

"Yes, you two lovebirds go ahead. I'll make our guest feel at home."

"This gesture means a lot to me," Theo told Gretchen. "Was it really Nate's idea?"

"Yes, he wanted to surprise you," she explained.

"You could've spared him and taken the credit," he said, smiling.

Gretchen simply smiled back and said, "I appreciate it. Thank you."

Theo backed up his gratitude with a soft kiss to Gretchen's

cheek. She closed her eyes and sighed. Gretchen and Theo were feeling a mutual bond developing between them and a sense of appreciation for each other. She accepted his invitation to sit with him in the family room.

"Well, this certainly feels like a dream to me."

Their eyes met as Gretchen reached for his hand as they sat on the sectional.

"I feel safe in this dream world with you," she said. "I wish I could stay here forever."

"You are welcome to stay for as long as you want, and I promise to keep you safe."

Gretchen saw the twinkle in Theo's eyes as her eyes wandered around the family room. She felt comfortable with his hospitality as he patiently waited until she became oriented. Gretchen felt assured that she was in good hands and fell in love with Theo's home. She noticed the immaculate condition of the family room. The floor was spotless, and a beautiful crystal chandelier hung over a fuchsia, blue, and teal area rug.

After a few silent moments, Gretchen's attention was drawn to some pictures on the wall. She walked over for a closer view.

Theo noticed the quizzical look on her face and came over, standing to her right as he explained, "That's Heather with me on one of our jogging trips. She was a long-distance runner, back in the day."

Gretchen's attention was drawn to four portraits mounted on the wall. She recognized Theo and Nate and was captivated by the picture of Heather and another with her, Theo, and Nate. She was quite attractive, with a dark-brown complexion, brown eyes, white teeth, and a beautiful smile.

"I see now why you're attracted to Bertha; she could pass for Heather's twin sister."

"I agree, and I see her in you too. Fuchsia was her favorite color."

"I must say that your deep affection for Bertha is amazing."

"What I find most interesting is how your story brought you to me. Is this just a coincidence?"

"I believe so," Gretchen said, "but as the song goes, it's not for me to say."

"Hmm. That's one of my favorite songs."

Theo could hear the tune and thought it would have been premature. Then he got back on track and in line with the conversation.

"You started writing your story long before I took some of those pictures; everything seemed so aligned, as if you were there. I remember sensing that something was wrong, and then I saw the broken guardrail on the bridge. It's starting to make sense but is still a mystery."

"That's why I need to dig deep into this mystery to discover the truth," Gretchen said.

"I can see that you are very determined," Theo observed.

Gretchen was encouraged by Theo's interest and positive attitude, although the look on his face indicated otherwise. She could understand his reluctance to be hopeful, but he was supportive of her. She became aware of his feeling of loneliness, his need to enhance his quality of life. He explained that he relied on his research studies to keep him busy, and he didn't do much socializing.

Theo was surprised to know that Gretchen had much the same routine and not enough time in the day for leisure. She said she used work and writing to distract herself from boredom. Theo became even more fascinated when he found out that she was a researcher, interested in further development of life satisfaction and attachment theories as they relate to young people. Theo believed that Gretchen was a phenomenal woman who was very passionate about serving humanity. However, he could sense that she tried to avoid talking about the sufferings in her life.

"I need to complete the work my Father has sent me to do, so that disenfranchised people's voices might be heard," she said.

"I believe that the devastation of innocent souls like Bertha's have gone unnoticed far too long, and the Creator has heard our hearts cry."

At that moment, Meemee entered the family room with two bottles of wine and glasses on a tray.

"Riesling or Lambrusco?" she offered.

"Lambrusco for me," said Theo.

"Same here," said Gretchen.

They watched as Meemee set the tray on the glass top center table, in front of the beige sectional where Theo and Gretchen sat. They watched as she poured the red wine into two wine glasses.

"I've noticed that you both have some things in common, among many, I suppose. You both like red wine. Enjoy."

They thanked Meemee for the compliment and resumed their conversation; she excused herself to rejoin Nate in the kitchen.

Gretchen's tour of Theo's family room was almost over. As they turned the corner, she could see a door that opened into the back patio. Her eyes were fixed on the study, on a platform to their left. Theo informed her this was his favorite place in the house. She noticed numerous books, encyclopedias, and journals on several shelves along the wall. A computer sat on a four-seater antique table in the center of the study.

As they walked back to the sectional sofa, Gretchen noticed two floral armchairs and a matching end table between them. A large TV was mounted on one wall, with a fireplace below. A large curio cabinet was in another corner, filled with trophies, porcelain statues, and other keepsakes.

A few minutes later, Theo and Gretchen were called to joined Nate and Meemee in the dining room, where the table was filled with beautiful birthday gifts, decorations, food, wine, and lots of other goodies. A lovely birthday cake with a number 70-shaped candle burned brightly in the middle.

Nate announced, "Today, August 25, 2017, Dad is celebrating

his seventieth birthday. We're all happy that Gretchen is here to share in this special moment with us. I thank you."

"My pleasure," she said.

"I am so proud of my gentle yet majestic dad."

Theo gave Nate a big hug.

"Happy birthday, Dad. I understand how important it is for you to see me happy, but your happiness is all that matters to me now."

"Thank you, son," said Theo.

He felt very happy and was even happier when Gretchen and Meemee joined in with their hugs.

"Thank you all for caring. This is a pleasant surprise and one of the best days of my life," Theo remarked.

"You've always told me that true happiness will come in due course," Nate said. "It is the outgrowth of patience. Thank you for being patient with me also. You are the best dad. I love you."

As they hugged, Theo replied, "I love you very much, Nateandro. Thank you for being the best son when I couldn't be the best dad."

"I must say a special thanks to Meemee for being a great support system," Nate continued. "Her parents could not be here today, but they've been very good to me for years, especially when Dad wasn't available, after Mom passed away."

Gretchen looked on and smiled.

"Thank you all so very much. I am happy knowing you all care about me.

"Theo, on the count of three: one, two, three."

He followed the hint and blew out the candle. They all cheered and sang along with Stevie Wonder's "Happy Birthday to You," the music playing in the background. Theo jigged to the beat, and his guests joined in and danced with him.

Theo thanked his guests and hugged everyone again. Then they gathered around as he opened his gifts, which included a white shirt, a blue and red striped tie, a portrait of Nate and Theo framed in gold, a black fleece robe with "Theo" embroidered on pocket, and a card saying "Theo, you've made your threescore-and-ten years. Happy 70th Birthday! With Love, Gretchen."

"I thank you, Nate, Meemee, and Gretchen for this splendid occasion. You've warmed my heart, and I love you all very much. Let's eat, drink, and be merry."

Gretchen was happy to see Theo in such a jolly mood. She noticed that he didn't take more than a couple sips from his glass of wine, just as much as she did. Nevertheless, she was certain that they all had a wonderful time listening to music, dancing, and chitchatting until close to midnight. When the party was over, Gretchen felt a bit sad, and she could see from Theo's face that he was sad as well. She was thrilled when Theo held her hand and walked her to Nate's car. Then Gretchen experienced the most loving thing:

"Dr. Gretchen Mocktruman," Theo began, "you are an interesting and beautiful person, and I would love to know you better." He kissed her lips softly and then opened the door for her.

Gretchen knew from that moment she was smitten and would have a dear friend in Theo.

"Dr. Theodorus Worlington, the feeling is mutual. Thank you for the warm welcome, and I'm looking forward to a lasting friendship with you."

"Everlasting," Gretchen heard him say.

They kissed again and said good night.

Theo saw to it that she was safely in her seat behind Meemee and then closed the door. Gretchen could hear Nate and Meemee saying good night again to Theo, who threw three kisses at them and then walked back to his front door. She could hear the engine throttling and saw the headlights on Theo as Nate waited for him to enter the house.

Gretchen noticed that someone was watching them from a window on the top floor of Miwa's house across the street. Then her attention returned to Nate backing the car out of the driveway and driving off.

The next evening, Gretchen decided to trade in her alone time for an evening out with Nate and Meemee at Chuck's Place, their favorite seafood and entertainment venue. Nate had spoken highly of Take Five Step, his band, which played at Chuck's, and Gretchen had agreed to meet them. She was aware that these musicians would be performing at the variety show in eight weeks.

They sat at a table for three to the left of the stage.

"The New England clam chowder was the best I've had in a long time," she told Nate and Meemee. "The grilled bluefish was even yummier."

Gretchen declined to have dessert and watched as they finished their key lime pie. She felt very relaxed in her fuchsia sweater and black pants. Nate looked very handsome in a gold satin shirt and black pants. Meemee's gold and black floral dress caught some attention too.

Nate introduced Gretchen to the owners of Chuck's Place, two older men named Sid and Chuck.

"How are you fellows doing?" Nate asked.

"Not as good as you, with two fine ladies next to you," Sid replied.

"I'm good," said Chuck.

"She's a good-looking black woman," Sid said, looking at Gretchen.

"I'll second that," said Chuck.

"I hope her English is as good as her looks," remarked Sid.

The performers in Take Five Step opened the show with an instrumental version of "A Summer Place." All the members were dressed in outfits the same as Nate's.

Gretchen was impressed by the band's professionalism, but

she felt a bit uneasy. She was reassured by Meemee, her little hostess, sitting beside her, and Nate was on her right, close to the aisle. Gretchen watched and listened as Chuck Jr. strummed his bass guitar as he introduced himself and the band members: Sid Jr. was on drums, Bobby played rhythm guitar, Martin was on keyboards, and Tyrone played saxophone.

Chuck Jr. added, "Ladies and gentlemen, the Take Five Steps band and Jenny Knorft, our new lead singer, welcome you to the show."

Jenny was very attractive with a fair complexion, curly black hair, and red lipstick, matching her shimmering red gown with gold strapped shoes. She strutted to center stage and bowed as she picked up the microphone.

"This song is dedicated to Nate and his fiancée, Meemee, and their guest, Gretchen. Welcome to Chuck's Place."

Gretchen did not see this coming and with a smile on her face lip-synced a "Thank you" and applauded with the rest of the audience.

Gretchen was delighted to see Nate take Meemee by the hand and led her onto the dance floor, below the stage. They got close and started moving to the beat of the prelude to the song "Danke Schoen."

The audience applauded wildly, wooing and whistling until Jenny started singing, "Danke Schoen, darling, Danke Schoen."

Gretchen listened and watched as Nate and Meemee increased their cadence. Then he gently pulled her close and whispered into her ear as Jenny sang, "Thank you for all the joy and pain."

Meemee blushed, and Jenny sang, "Picture show, second balcony, was the place we'd meet."

Gretchen got up to videotape the couple as they waltzed. The spotlight was back on Jenny as she continued singing, "Danke Schoen, oh darling, Danke Schoen."

Gretchen noticed a suspicious-looking man standing at the bar. He had a tanned complexion and a red bandana tied around his head. His black hair was shoulder length. He was leaning on the bar and chatting with the bartender. The suspicious man had his menacing eyes fixed on Nate and Meemee on the dance floor. He took a couple sips from his glass of beer and kept looking at his watch.

Gretchen kept videotaping the dancing couple, but she was also feeling very uneasy. Her focus was distracted by Jenny singing the last line of the song: "Auf wiedersehen."

Then she curtsied, threw the audience a kiss, and glided off the stage.

Gretchen noticed that the suspicious man had walked over to an unoccupied table across the aisle from where she sat with Nate and Meemee, who had returned to their seats. The man took out his cell phone, looked at the screen, and put the phone back in his pocket. He became uneasy when he caught Chuck and Sid staring at him. As Meemee positioned in the aisle, cell phone in hand, to take a picture of Jenny singing, the man almost tripped over her. She clicked a snapshot of him by accident.

Gretchen saw Nate as he rushed to Meemee's side and watched as the man hurried down the aisle and ran out the front door. Gretchen comforted Meemee; Nate asked if she wanted to leave, but she wanted to stay, and so did Meemee.

"I'm okay," Gretchen and Meemee said, almost in unison.

On regaining his composure, Nate rejoined the band on stage. He played his violin as the band performed another instrumental, "Stranger on the Shore." It was such a calming moment for Gretchen, who was having flashbacks of Bertha on life support in the hospital bed. Gretchen's attention was drawn back to Chuck's Place when Nate took a moment to introduce her. She was teary-eyed as she heard the audience cheering.

"Welcome, Miss Gretchen! I hope your time in Vanityville will be great."

Gretchen heard whistles and clapping all around her. Meemee gave Gretchen a big hug as she wiped away her tears.

It was such a memorable moment for her and lingered in her mind even long after the show.

I feel so much love here, she thought. *I sense a kind of mother-daughter bond developing between Meemee and me. I'm happy she confided in me about her concern that Nate was involved with some bad people.*

Chapter 7

That same evening, Theo was preoccupied, sitting behind his prized antique desk in his cozy little office. He had just finished listening to the taped conversation he had with Colanda and decided to prepare himself for his next appointment. Then Theo was distracted by thoughts Gretchen enjoying herself at Chuck's Place with Nate and Meemee. He glanced at her picture in his cellphone and felt as if he was looking at Heather.

A knock on the door brought him back, and on his security monitor, Theo could see Drake, his nephew, standing outside his door. He let him in, and they hugged.

"Thanks for showing up," he said. "Please have a seat."

Drake's tall, athletic stature reminded Theo of his brother, Earl, Drake's father.

"I'd like to have a heart-to-heart discussion with you," he announced, watching Drake as he walked over and sat in the armchair in front of his desk.

"Why today?" Drake asked.

"Your mother called me a few minutes ago," Theo replied, "pouring her heart out about the issues you both are having, and I'd like to hear what you have to say."

"I can't talk about what's in my heart," Drake said. "I only need to get away from here for a while. I need to start taking care of me."

"I understand, but I'd like to hear your answer to one question: do you treat your mother with disrespect?"

"Everyone's upset with me because I speak my mind. I don't mean to disrespect her."

"If you speak your mind with respect, then that's okay. If not, it's a problem. Being disrespectful to your mother is not acceptable."

"I get blamed for everything, even if I stick up for Mom against Berba. So I have to distance myself."

"You think distancing yourself will be a solution to your issues? Where would you go?"

"I got an offer to play guitar with a band out of state. It's a steady job."

"You need stability in your life, but that won't solve the problems you have with others. What does your mother think about this plan of yours?"

"She doesn't care about me," Drake snapped. "She spends most of her time fighting with Berba."

"Your mom's dating him?"

"She said he was a family friend back when my dad was alive."

Theo recalled seeing the red pickup truck in Colanda's driveway.

"Does Berba drive a red pickup truck?"

"I think so," Drake said. "Why?"

"I've seen it parked in Colanda's driveway and was curious."

"Well, he parks his truck there quite a bit, sometimes for days when he goes out of town with one of his buddies. He drives a black van then. He returns later to take his frustrations out on Mom, arguing about the slightest thing. I get very upset when he yells at her. That's why I must leave this town, before somebody gets hurt."

"Are you planning to hurt someone?" Theo asked gently.

"I'm not really planning, but if he tries to hurt my mother or me, I won't just stand there and do nothing."

"Drake, is there anything else bothering you?"

"I'm not sure what's going on, but one night, I went home and found Mom in bed, crying. I saw Berba standing over her, yelling at her. She said she wasn't feeling well, but he kept on yelling. He said he was sick too, sick of listening to her. Then he started talking bad about me, saying that I was out of control and causing trouble all the time. I heard him say that he was trying not to put his hands on me. I have some of it on tape," Drake said. "Listen."

He played back the conversation he'd recorded on his cell phone.

"I'll be fine. It's just a little twenty-four-hour bug bothering me. Please don't take this out on him. He misses his dad and is going through a lot. He doesn't have any close friends."

"It's about time you realize that boy won't change and stop taking sides with him against me. Can't you see that he has no regard for anything you do? He doesn't respect you."

"Berba, listen to yourself talk. You are no different. Why don't you set a better example for him to follow?"

"Don't make me shut you up."

Drake stopped the tape and explained, "He was yelling at Mom, and I wanted to go in there and take him on, but I decided not to because I knew he had a gun. I started knocking things around, so he got even more upset, stormed out of the room, and drove away. Mom said she was glad I came home, and I told her I was sorry for the things I've said."

"How old are you, Drake?" Theo asked.

"I'll be twenty-four in a couple months."

"You are a very good storyteller and wise beyond your years. You handled the situation well. I believe you. I know you and Colanda are both hurting. My brother was a good father and husband, but now he's gone."

"I know, and that's the problem. I want to be there for Mom, but that dude is in the way. No one believes me when I speak the truth. Yet everything others say about me behind my back is believed to be the truth."

"Drake, I understand your frustrations, but don't let the wrongs that others do to you change who you are. You continue to do the right thing and speak the truth. Don't worry; I'm here for you. Thanks for telling me your story. I'll follow up with your mom."

"I thank you, Uncle Theo. You're the only one who has something good to say about me."

"You're welcome. Come here, son."

Drake threw himself into Theo's outreached arms, and they hugged each other.

———◇———

About thirty minutes after Drake left the office, Theo noticed an incoming call on his cell phone. It was his nephew.

"Hi, Drake. I'm just packing up to leave. May I call you back in about fifteen minutes?"

Theo listened and then announced, "What? Who could've done such a thing?"

Theo paced the floor, a look of terror on his face as he continued to listen.

"Are the paramedics there?"

Theo could hear Drake breathing heavily and realized that he was at a loss for words, stammering as he spoke.

"They are here n-n-now, working on h-h-her," he said.

"Okay, I'll be there as quickly as I can. Don't leave," Theo instructed while walking briskly toward the door.

Theo rushed to his Bentley, parked in the basement. Inside the car, he calmed down a little after he heard the engine throttling. Feeling safely buckled in, he backed the car out of the parking lot, drove off, and headed north on Gentry Cove Freeway. He tried to stay calm and concentrate on his driving. After a moment's silence, he could hear the words echoing in his head.

"Colanda's dead! Mom is dead."

"I can't believe it. I talked to her about an hour ago," Theo said.

Many questions entered his mind, the first of which provoked a dreaded possibility. *Could Drake have killed his mother? Was he correct about Berba's abusive treatment? Could Berba have killed her? How can I help in this situation? What else did I do wrong? What's going to happen next?*

Theo was quite distraught, and as he drove in silence, he could see the marina ahead, his landmark for knowing he was near Colanda and Drake's home. As he turned left onto Marshvalley Circle, he noticed a police car parked at the third house on the left. He saw an ambulance in Colanda's driveway and yellow crime scene tape. Theo pulled over and tried to calm himself down.

"I can't believe it," he repeated. "Colanda is dead, gone."

Theo sat in his car and watched as the EMTs wheeled a gurney toward the back of the ambulance. He noticed a shrouded body strapped to the gurney. He continued to watch while trying to hold back the tears when he saw the gurney being lifted into the ambulance. Seconds later, the ambulance drove away. It reminded him of the night Bertha was wheeled away from the creek, not too far up the road. The difference, he recalled, was Bertha was still alive when that ambulance drove away.

"I should've listened to Colanda, my best instinct, and visited her. Things might have been different if I had acted earlier. Colanda, I am so sorry. Please forgive me," Theo whispered as he took out his cell phone and texted, "Drake, I'm outside."

As Theo approached the front door, he noticed Drake standing there to let him in. As they embraced, Theo could hear Drake sobbing, and his tears were flowing too. About a minute later, Theo noticed two police officers walking toward the door.

He recognized them instantly as the two officers who had given him a ride home the night of Bertha's accident. He greeted them with a handshake and informed them that he was Drake's uncle.

"We are sorry about your loss, sir," Officer Gabriel said.

"Our thoughts are with you," Officer Rafael said. "Please let us know if we can help."

Drake broke down crying again as Theo hugged him tighter.

"I g-g-got home to find her in bed, a pillow over her f-f-face." Drake's voice stammered while he spoke. "I couldn't save her, Uncle Theo. Why couldn't I save her?"

Theo could identify with Drake's grief while trying to manage his.

"Drake, it's not your fault," he said.

He made eye contact with Drake, who quickly wiped away his tears.

Theo continued, "You did the best you could. Your mom would never blame you, and I am here for you."

The silence told Theo that Drake was processing what he'd just said. He could feel Drake holding him tight as he sobbed. Then when the sobbing stopped, Theo told Drake he could stay in his house until they figured what the next step should be. Drake accepted.

Theo watched Drake run up the stairs to get his belongings. Meanwhile, he sat on the sofa, opposite the front door.

Then his attention was drawn to the portrait of Earl, Colanda, and Drake, hanging on the wall between the windows. Each picture was in a decorative frame with the name printed below. Another portrait hung on the wall; "Bertha" was written below it.

Theo could hear his heart pounding in his chest as he remembered Bertha's pictures that Gretchen had showed him.

"Is our Bertha Colanda's mother?" he asked himself.

He quickly dismissed the question and managed to remain calm as he took snapshots of all the portraits. Then he decided to take pictures of all the furniture, ornaments, and portraits in Colanda's living room.

He heard Drake's footsteps and called out to him.

"Drake, make sure all the doors and windows are locked up there. I'll see to the ones down here."

"Got it," Drake shouted back, and seconds later, he joined his uncle in the living room.

All the windows were secured on the top floor; Theo watched as Drake locked his Honda Civic parked in the driveway.

They got into his Bentley, and Theo backed out of the driveway. He noticed that Drake was looking back at his home as it faded in the distance. Theo could see the sad look on Drake's face, and he felt the same way in his heart as he drove in silence. Five minutes later, Theo pulled his Bentley into his driveway. He thanked Drake for accepting his offer to spend some time with him, and as they walked toward the front door, he became quite pensive.

This is the second time I'll be responsible for a life that's traumatized, he thought. *Yet the worst feeling is not knowing how to handle this complicated situation.*

Several hours later, Theo was awakened by the buzzing on his cell phone. He quickly reached for the phone, thinking it was Gretchen, who he had been trying to contact all day. Instead, he noticed the Med Center on his cell screen. He could feel his heart beating fast as he answered the call.

"Hello? Hello?"

He waited but realized there was no response, and he had no choice but to hang up.

Whoever it is will call again, he thought but had a strange feeling that something was wrong.

He looked over to the other lounge chair and saw Drake lying there, sound asleep. Theo had invited him to sit with him on the back patio. They'd had a light snack, and both had been relaxing on lounge chairs when they fell asleep.

We needed to sleep, he told himself. *I'm feeling energized and ready to go again.*

Then he noticed two missed calls and two missed text messages, one from Gretchen and one from Meemee. He decided to try again and quickly clicked on Gretchen's number.

"Went to her voicemail again," he said aloud. He decided to wait for a minute and then clicked her number again.

"Voicemail."

Then he decided to try calling Meemee. He clicked her number and could not get through to her, either.

"Voicemail again. Hmm," he said, feeling very concerned.

Chapter 8

Gretchen made another attempt to connect with Theo. Still no response.

My call went straight to his voicemail, she thought. *Very strange.*

Then she noticed the name MEEMEE on her cell screen. She was calling from the hospital, and Gretchen was very happy to hear that Nate's surgery went well. Yet she remained concerned that Theo could not be reached. It was after midnight, and Meemee had not heard from Theo, after making several attempts to contact him.

Gretchen was not able to reach Leo either, so she decided to call it a day, telling Meemee that she'd visit Nate later in the day. Gretchen listened and then replied, "I'll try calling his cell one more time. If there's no response, we should report him missing, even though it's not quite twenty-four hours yet."

She listened again and replied, "Love you too. Get some sleep."

Gretchen pressed END, waited a couple minutes, and then dialed Theo's number.

"Line busy," she said. "At least that might be a good sign. I'll keep trying."

Then a couple minutes later, Gretchen could hear her phone ringing and was beyond relieved when she saw the name THEO. She pressed the green button and said a quick "Thank you, God."

"Ditto," she could hear Theo respond; he had wondered where she was all day.

"I've been trying to reach you for several hours. Where have you been?" Gretchen asked.

She could hear the sobbing and realized that Theo must have heard about Nate. She remained still and waited for Theo to respond.

"I've heard about Nate from Meemee. Thank you, Gretchen, and sorry about the missed calls. I'm with Drake. Get some sleep, and text me the time you need to be picked up tomorrow."

Gretchen became tearful as she heard Theo's grief-stricken voice. She could feel his pain, having to deal with the tragic news about his sister-in-law and his son's near-death experience, both in one day.

———◇———

The next morning, Gretchen stopped to buy a bouquet of flowers from the gift shop in the hospital lobby after she arrived with Theo and Drake.

Gretchen led the way to Intensive Care Unit Room 7, with Theo and Drake following closely behind her. As she entered the room, Gretchen saw that Nate was awake but looking groggy. She noticed his leg was lifted in traction.

"Hi, Gretchen, good to see you. Where is Dad?"

"I'm right here," Theo said as he walked in.

Gretchen set the large bouquet of flowers on the end table to Nate's right, gave him a hug, and then noticed as Theo and Drake followed behind her. In that moment, Gretchen felt sorrow mingled with gladness as she listened and watched the reactions. She glanced at the clock on the wall behind the TV, which showed 10:45.

"Nate, I'm so sorry for not making it here earlier," Theo said. "I've been with Drake the whole time."

"Dad, I understand, and I feel better knowing you were there for Drake. I saw it on TV a few minutes ago about your mom," Nate said, looking at Drake.

Gretchen realized that this was too much for Drake, who started to sob as he walked quickly out of the room, and so she decided to follow him.

This is my golden opportunity to get to know him better, she thought.

She noticed that Drake had stopped to wait for her, and on getting up to where he stood, she asked, "Is it okay for me to stand by you for a few minutes?"

"Yes, Miss Gretchen," he said. "I'm okay with you."

"Let me know if you need something or if I can help in any way."

"Thank you," he said. "That's nice of you. Right now, I don't feel like I belong here. I must find a place to go, maybe out of state."

That was a gut-wrenching moment for her too. Her tears flowed, and she knew that Drake saw them, but it didn't matter. All she wanted to do was hug him, and he hugged her. Together, they sobbed, just a little. Then she noticed Drake stepping away as he spoke.

"Miss Gretchen, my mother brought me here, and now she is gone."

She heard him sob a little more and stammering as he spoke again.

"All I ever wanted in my twenty-four years is to feel I belonged."

Gretchen kept silent. How well she understood as she walked over and held him close, then spoke.

"Drake, if this will make a difference in how you feel, please know that I am here for you."

Then Gretchen could feel someone else's arms across her right shoulder; she turned around and looked up into Theo's baby-blue eyes. She could see his tears. Their hearts were overwhelmed as they hugged Drake.

"You guys make me feel jealous. May I join in?" Gretchen recognized Meemee's voice as she approached. There was a big circle of huggers, and Gretchen noticed that even Drake was smiling.

"Good to see you again, Meemee," he said.

"Same here, Drake," she replied and then walked over and gave him a hug.

"Happy to have you, Drake."

"Me too. Thanks," he said.

Gretchen could see Theo smiling.

"Such a beautiful array. I thank you all," she said.

She huddled everyone together, and they quickly posed for a selfie.

Then beckoning to them, she announced, "Let's get back to Nate. He must be wondering where we are."

"He dozed off again," Theo reported.

"He's pretty doped up," Meemee said, "getting painkillers around the clock."

As they neared Nate's room, Gretchen could see him sitting up in bed, watching TV. Meemee and Theo were the first through the door and at his bedside. They took turns, Meemee going first to hug and smooch him. Then Theo gave him a high five and kissed his forehead.

"Good to see you more alive," he said.

Then Drake stepped up to greet Nate, right after Gretchen gave Nate a hug and kiss on the forehead.

"Hey, bro, nice to see you again, though sad that it had to be like this," said Drake.

"Good to see you, Drake. It's been about two years since I saw you, and it was during an altercation."

"Well, I've changed since then; I'm so sorry to have called you nappy head. I was only lashing out at you for getting between me and my friend Bobby. I can't even remember what had happened."

"Yeah, man, let bygones be bygones. Again, I'm so sorry about your loss—our loss. We're family, bro. I'm sorry," Nate said, his voice trembling.

Gretchen was overjoyed at the outcome. Drake was stooping down at the bedside and resting his head on Nate's chest, while Nate gently patted his back. Drake got up and walked back to stand beside Theo, who was wiping the tears from his eyes.

"Thanks, Drake. Your presence is truly felt in this room," Nate declared.

"Presence?" Drake remarked.

"Nate, this is the very room that Bertha was put in when she was admitted here in August," Theo interjected.

"What a coincidence," Nate exclaimed.

"I've also discovered that Bertha may be Colanda's mother. I have pictures."

Theo pulled up the snapshots in his cell—portrait pictures of Bertha, Colanda, Earl, and Drake—and showed them to Nate. Luckily, Gretchen was already sitting in the recliner opposite Nate's bed; otherwise, she would have passed out when Theo broke the news.

"Surreal," Nate exclaimed as he scrutinized the snapshot with the names engraved at the bottom of each person's portrait.

"Am I to believe that the strange woman who disappeared from here is Grandma Bertha? No way." Drake shook his head in disbelief.

It was Gretchen's turn to look at the snapshots, and she had to agree with Theo's hunch.

"Surely, Drake, my dearly beloved and best friend Bertha is your grandmother."

All the others joined in unanimously.

"You look like both your parents," Meemee said, "and I can see a little of Bertha in your smile and very caring nature."

"This is truly a memorable day in all our lives, and I am truly grateful to have you as my family members," Nate announced. "To change the subject a little, it's possible that I'll be going to rehab in a few days. My orthopedic doctor feels I'm making remarkable progress, but I need about six weeks of physical therapy."

"Thank God for that," Drake said.

"I don't mean to upset anyone, but why were you shot?" Drake asked. "What did you do?"

Gretchen noticed Nate looking at her and Theo, and before anyone could say anything, he responded, "I am still trying to process what happened, but I know it took a miracle. Maybe Meemee and Gretchen can tell us more."

"Are you sure you want us to talk about it now?" Theo asked, and she noticed that Nate's response brought tears to everybody's eyes.

"Don't worry, y'all. I would like to know too. What did I do to deserve this? Who was so wicked to have shot me? God knows I can handle talking about it."

Gretchen could hear Nate's voice breaking as he sobbed, trying to get the words out.

She walked over to his bedside and held his hand while Theo and Drake drew closer, standing next to her. She noticed that Meemee was at Nate's left side, gently wiping the tears from his eyes and stroking his forehead while she spoke.

"Nate, you've done nothing wrong," Meemee said. "Sometimes the Creator may use evil to point us to the path we must follow."

Nate said, "Meemee, please tell us what happened."

"I didn't see everything; it happened so fast, one thing leading into another. Gretchen, Nate, and I had just left Chuck's Place and stopped by the community center auditorium, where the show will be held. Gretchen had left us to use the restroom. I was sitting at the piano on stage. Nate was singing along with me as I played 'The Love of God,' a timeless treasure."

She recalled their voices singing:

The love of God, how rich, how pure
how measureless and strong.

It shall forevermore endure
the saints and angels' song.

"Our voices were echoing throughout the empty auditorium, when we heard a door slam behind the stage. I stopped playing as we listened. Then Nate called out, saying, 'Who's there?' but we didn't hear a response. Nate told me to stay there at the piano while he went to check if anyone was back there."

"That is correct," Nate said, "and what happened after that is coming back to me now." He tried to pull himself up to a sitting position in the bed.

Gretchen and Meemee assisted in raising the bed and repositioning the pillow under his head. He held Meemee's hand as she sat beside him in the bed, and he continued to speak.

"I walked into a room backstage; it was poorly lit, but it was clear enough for me to see a tall figure in a black hooded outfit exiting the door. By the time I got to the door, the figure was about twenty-five feet down the pathway leading to the annex. In a split-second, I heard an explosion and felt an excruciating pain in my hip. I screamed and fell to the ground; I couldn't move. I felt like the room was spinning and started blacking out. I could hear a voice saying, 'Don't leave us, Nate. Meemee and Gretchen are here with you, and we need you to take some deep breaths. Breathe, breathe.'

"I tried, but I couldn't. I could see blackness, and the pain had gotten worse. Then I felt a pressure on top of my hand, and that revived me a bit."

"That's the part I didn't know," Meemee interjected. "I heard a terrifying scream, like someone in pain. I was petrified but managed to shout, 'Nate! Nate! Are you okay?' but there was no answer. So I took out my cell phone, dialed 911, and told them we needed an ambulance at the community center. In my gut, I felt that Nate was in danger. I called Theo—no answer—but was happy when I saw Gretchen returning. She said she had heard the scream, and she noticed that Nate was not with me. She ran past me; by the time I got to the back door, Gretchen was already at Nate's side."

Gretchen joined in to report that she'd done a quick assessment and noticed that Nate was holding his left side, and his shirt was saturated with blood. He was lying on his left side and groaning, as if in severe pain. She turned him slightly to the right and quickly applied direct pressure on top of his left hand on his hip. Meemee was stooping over Nate, his head on her leg, and talking to him while wiping sweat from his forehead. She reported to Gretchen that he was breathing and followed her instructions. Meemee kept Nate's head from moving and encouraged him to take one or two deep breaths.

"In through your nose and let it out, slowly, through your mouth. It will help to relieve the pain."

Gretchen noticed that the grimace on Nate's face was gone. His groaning had subsided.

He took another deep breath and let it out slowly. "Thank you, Jesus," Meemee said.

"Nate, one more deep breath," Meemee continued. "Can you point and flex your right foot?"

He did.

Meemee looked sad when Nate couldn't do the same with his left foot.

Then Gretchen heard sirens blaring. "Stay with us, Nate," she said. "The ambulance is here."

Seconds later, the paramedics arrived and took over rescue operations. Gretchen saw them moving very quickly to administer first aid. Nate was awake; his eyes were opened. They used a long board to transfer him onto a gurney. He was strapped down and the gurney wheeled into the rear of the ambulance. Gretchen and Meemee were relieved as they watched the ambulance driving off with Nate and heard sirens wailing.

"Thank you so much, Meemee and Gretchen, for saving my life. I found out later that I was given two units of blood during surgery. A bullet was removed from my left hip. No nerve damage, and I'll definitely walk again. Thank God," Nate said.

Gretchen noticed that Theo was looking very distraught, at a loss for words. She admired his strength of character and how much he adored Nate but had also taken the time to grieve with Drake and be there for all of them.

"Losing Heather and my brother and then dealing with Colanda's demise and Bertha's disappearance—wow. It would be too much for us all to bear if Nate was taken also, but God knows best," Theo murmured.

"Speaking of Mom," Nate said, "I thought I was looking at her when I opened my eyes and saw Miss Gretchen in that fuchsia and black outfit. I was so happy to see her. I remember a warm feeling in my hip and down my leg, and I was not hurting that much after she applied pressure.

"You did look like Nate's Mom," Meemee said as she nodded in agreement.

"I agree also," Theo said.

"Thank you, Mom," Nate exclaimed.

Gretchen could feel the sincere gratitude and replied, "Thank you, son."

"Ooh! So sweet," Meemee said, as she hugged Gretchen on Nate's behalf. "This is the closest I've come to realizing how truly precious life is. I know everything happens for a reason but losing Nate would be extremely difficult for me to accept."

Gretchen nodded in agreement as Meemee turned to Drake, held his hands and continued, "Drake, I can only imagine what you are going through. Please don't hesitate to let us know how we may be of help. I'm glad you are here with us."

"Thank you, Meemee. I'm happy to have you guys. I feel much better, just being here and knowing Nate will be okay," Drake said.

"Let's pray, guys," said Nate, and Gretchen beckoned to everyone to come closer. They all gathered around.

"Heavenly Father, we thank you."

Chapter 9

In the early morning of the next day, Gretchen was awake and feeling very comfortable in pink pajamas, her hair in two braids down to her shoulders. As she lay on the queen-size bed in Theo's guest room, her eyes were closed in meditation, thinking how blessed she was to have met Theo, especially at a time when death was closing in. He had made her feel like a pampered child with everything she ever wished for in life, completely satisfied.

Gretchen also thought that Theo had handled himself very well. She saw him as a perfect gentleman, even under adverse circumstances.

Theo knocked on her door and reported the news that Colanda's body had disappeared from the morgue.

"I was informed by the medical examiner that autopsy was not done," he said.

Gretchen jumped off the bed to join him on the way to Drake's room.

She followed behind him as he walked hurriedly across the upstairs loft to Drake's room. They found the door open and the bed empty but made, as if it had not been slept in.

Gretchen walked over to the open window and saw a ladder against the outer side of the house. She felt a little relief, thinking that Drake might have sneaked out.

"Drake hasn't answered my calls or text messages, either," Theo announced as he walked over to join her at the window.

The same thought was going through his mind as he hugged her. She could hear his sighs amid the silence. Shortly after, Gretchen followed Theo down the stairs to the family room, and as they sat on the sofa, he called Drake's cell phone again.

"Still no answer."

Theo decided to wait a few more minutes and then drive down to Colanda's house, if he didn't hear from his nephew.

Gretchen listened as Theo told her about his discussion with Colanda the day before she died. She had called his office and reported that she was having a very difficult time with Drake. He was constantly disrespectful to her and blamed Berba as the cause of their problem. She described Berba's role as a family friend who assisted them when Earl was still battling cancer.

She also reported that the red pickup truck belonged to Oscar, Berba's friend. She confirmed that Berba had a beard and was a very unpleasant character. Theo had planned to go to Colanda's home for a follow-up visit with her and Drake, but she died the day before.

"I am so sorry that I wasn't paying closer attention after Earl died," Theo said. "Colanda, please forgive me."

"Don't be hard on yourself," Gretchen said. "I'm sure you would've done something to remedy the situation, had you known. Please know, you are not alone in this. I'm here to support you."

He was appreciative but took responsibility for his failure to be more vigilant on Colanda's behalf. Gretchen was in shock when Theo told her of his findings: Berba was Skip's half-brother by his mother's side. Skip had claimed to be Colanda's legal representative with complete control over her insurance benefits, as surviving spouse of Earl, Theo's deceased brother.

The motive behind Colanda's and Bertha's disappearance became a greater concern to Theo. Besides, he had discovered that it was not unusual for poor people to go missing. The reason he believed was due to their inability to afford proper burial. They were often buried in paupers' graves in Vanityville. Gretchen wanted to know where those graveyards were, but Theo did not know.

At that moment, he saw a text from Drake, saying he'd be home in a couple minutes.

Five minutes later, Drake was sitting in the family room on the sectional, with Theo and Gretchen to his left. They listened attentively as Drake told his story. He apologized for leaving without letting them know, but he didn't want to wake them up. He had felt the need to go down to his home and decided to sneak away using the ladder.

"I walked all the way home. It took me maybe about ten minutes. I got there about four o'clock in the morning and found Mom's house empty, except for these three portraits that I took down from the wall." Drake handed the pictures to Theo.

"My car was right where I left it, in Mom's driveway. I called the police and reported the robbery. They came and took fingerprints, and I filed a report and gave them Mom's letter."

He also said he gave Colanda's letter to the police but believed there wouldn't be a follow-up. He explained that he was upset and decided to stay at the house, by himself, for a while. Then he visited with his friend Bobby, the guitar player in Take Five Steps.

Theo realized that the worst part of Drake's grieving was that not much was done to bring the perpetrators to justice. He decided to read salient parts of Colanda's letter—a snapshot of the original, which Drake had texted him.

"Berba, you are the most despicable person I know, and I won't tolerate your abuse anymore. I was devastated and afraid when Earl died, so I reached out to you, thinking you had my family's best interest at heart. I thought I could trust you as a friend of the family. You were only seeking to help yourself at my family's expense. My home became a harbor. I kept silent for ten years. I am still a grieving widow and very suspicious that you may be involved with my mother's disappearance. Therefore, I want you out of my family's life, immediately!

"Colanda."

Gretchen and Theo eventually told Drake about his mom's body disappearing from the morgue. They could see the look of sadness on each other's face, and being stricken by grief, they hugged and comforted each other. Gretchen was starting to feel that it was more than she could bear, but her faith and the love surrounding her brought new hope and strength. She noticed that Drake looked surprised when he saw the wicker handbag on the table; the hospital staff had given it to Theo.

"That's Grandma Bertha's handbag," he exclaimed, and he was even more surprised when Gretchen took the white handkerchief with the letter C from the handbag.

"That's the handkerchief Mom gave Grandma Bertha."

"Yes, Drake, that's true," Gretchen said as the reality started to sink in, and they sat sorrowing in silence for a moment.

Then Gretchen continued to remove the other contents from Bertha's purse: a pair of black ballet shoes, denim pants, and a fuchsia T-shirt. Gretchen recalled her wearing this outfit when she saw Bertha at Dreamersville Hotel. She noticed the words "Bertha" and "Resurrected Gentry" printed on the front and back of the shirt.

Their attention had been drawn to Colanda's portrait that Theo was holding. Gretchen thought her flawless tanned skin, oval face, and alluring hazel eyes were like Drake's. Her curly brown hair and beautiful smile were like Bertha's. Gretchen believed that Colanda was the Mona Lisa of Vanityville, but more importantly, she was the Creator's purified, refined gem who was ready for the rapture and reunion. As Theo held up Earl's picture, Gretchen believed she was looking at a mirror image of himself, except Earl was younger of course and a little lighter in complexion.

Gretchen and Theo listened and were stunned when Drake reported that the last time when he saw Grandma Bertha, she was wearing a purple dress and black, low-heeled shoes. She was picked up by someone in a black Lexus on Friday night, and he heard the next day on the news about the car crash. Drake had a funny feeling it was her, but his mom was convinced it wasn't. The news had reported that Bertha had been driving a white car.

"Grandma Bertha doesn't drive, so no one who knows that would believe it was her driving that car," Drake explained, but he was not willing to discuss further.

A week later, September 2, 2017, Gretchen visited with Stefan and Monica Knorft, parents of Jenny, the new singer in the Take Five Steps band. Gretchen realized during her visit with the Knorfts that she was slowly becoming immersed into the culture of silence. She was not likely to talk about events and characters, even in her dreams.

Gretchen was feeling a little uneasy. She sat down next to Monica on a brown sofa. Monica was a very attractive woman, with a fair complexion and black curly hair. Gretchen watched as Monica reached for the remote control and switched off the TV. She noticed that Stefan had made himself comfortable on a barstool in the kitchen behind the sectional.

"I can see who Jenny got her pretty looks from. She looks a lot like you, Monica."

"Thank you. I used to have a difficult time keeping the boys away until Stefan showed up and swept me off my feet. He's much better now, not so upset when they look at me."

"I'm too busy working to notice," Stefan remarked.

Gretchen became more curious as she watched the interaction between the couple.

"On a serious note," Stefan said, "I told Jenny that I wanted to speak with you when she told me about the man at Chuck's Place the night you were there a week ago. Monica and I had watched the news on TV about the shooting that nearly took Nate's life."

"This neighborhood is certainly going to the dogs. I never

believed that I'd live to see the day when someone is shot right outside my door," said Monica.

"What's so special about this neighborhood? Bad people live here too," Stefan responded.

"It wasn't like this ten years ago."

"So what brought about the change?" Stefan asked.

"All sorts of people moving in, disturbing the peace, and setting bad examples for our children," Monica responded.

Stefan continued, "You mean it was other people's bad influence on our Jenny that got her singing in a nightclub?"

"Chuck's Place is not a nightclub," Monica corrected him. "Decent people go there to eat, have a drink, dance, and listen to music."

"And would you say the same for a strip club? Jenny worked there too," Stefan continued.

"Jenny didn't go back to Oohlia's after I talked some sense into her."

"It just goes to say how much you know about the people in your so-called good neighborhood. Or your daughter Jenny. Plus, did you know that the Worlington boy, a role model, was shot by a white person who blamed the shooting on a Native American? You ought to stop seeing people as black and white, bad and good, in that order. Get real, woman, times have not changed. People are more accepting of reality and willing to speak the truth now, or have they, Monica?"

Gretchen could feel the tension in the silence, which was broken by Stefan.

"Sorry about that. All I wanted to tell you is that you must be careful. A bald white man with a bushy beard rung my doorbell yesterday evening, asking for you. He said he was delivering a package Skip had sent you. He seemed suspicious and didn't say his name, so I didn't give him your address. He apologized about the mix-up and left. I didn't see any package in his hand. I watched as he drove away in a black van."

"I would never think that somebody like you would associate with that white man," Monica said. "He is a disgrace to the white race."

"There you go again," Stefan said to Monica as he handed two pictures to Gretchen.

"I don't know this bald guy, but I know Skip."

"I mean the disgraceful one named Skip. Isn't he a director at the center?" Monica asked.

"I don't know him that well for him to surprise me with a package," Gretchen responded, feeling a bit troubled.

Gretchen thanked Stefan for the snapshot of the bearded man and his black van and for warning her about Skip. She glanced at the two pictures and put them in her purse. She could hear Stefan apologize for arguing with Monica in her presence but made light of it. As Gretchen stepped outside, Monica closed the door behind her. She thought about taking another look at the picture but changed mind. Instead, she hurried home.

When she got home, Gretchen told Theo about her visit with the Knorfts and the warning she received.

"So Berba must be the bald-beaded, bearded one and Butch the bald-headed without a beard," Gretchen heard Theo say as he scrutinized the snapshot. She was taken by surprise when Theo suggested that she stay at his house until she'd found another place. He believed that it was dangerous for her to stay in Skip's apartment. She also felt that being closer to Drake would give her the opportunity to offer support and get to know him better.

Later, Theo challenged Gretchen to a game of Chinese checkers. They played at the table in the study, and Drake came over to watch. He sat on the chair to Theo's left and facing her. Gretchen listened as Theo informed Drake that he was no match for her; she had him beaten in all four games.

"Four games to none for Uncle Theo. You are a pro, Miss Gretchen. Could you teach me to play sometime?"

"Of course. I won't mind making you a pro too."

Gretchen decided to opt out and guide Drake as he played with Theo, and to their surprise, he had Theo down two games to one, in practice.

"You are a fast learner like your grandma Bertha, who taught me to play," she remarked.

"Nice! Sorry, Uncle Theo," Drake said.

Gretchen noticed a look of excitement on Drake's face when he got a text message on his cell.

"It's from Daisy," he said. "She emailed me the itinerary for my flight to San Diego tomorrow. Things are really moving fast."

"Don't you think it is a little too fast?" Theo asked.

"Better too fast than too slow. The faster I get myself situated in a job, the better for me. Plus, I'll have Mom, Grandma Bertha, and Dad watching over me, along with you."

Gretchen could see the sad but determined look on Drake's face. She felt very happy to know that he was ready to face challenges, despite the tragedies in his life. She agreed with him that the spirits of his relatives were watching over him. She had no doubt that the Creator had many blessings in store for him.

Theo also arranged for Drake's car to be shipped to him later and promised to watch over his mom's property and other belongings, like the portraits. He saw to a smooth transition; Drake was very impressed with the wisdom he demonstrated.

"I'll do all I can to help you," Theo said.

"I must keep my mind clear and focus on getting ahead and becoming self-sufficient," he said. "Daisy helped me get the job playing guitar in a band. She was my high school girlfriend and knows how good I am at the guitar; she thought about me when she saw a job listed in the paper. I'm not going to lie; I kinda like her still, but I won't be rushing into any serious relationship for a while."

"Please text me Daisy's address and phone number," Theo said, "in case I can't get ahold of you."

"I think that's a good plan. I will let her know," Drake concurred, and Theo was satisfied.

The next day was chilly and somber for Theo and Gretchen. They made sure that Drake got to the airport on time. They waved as the plane to San Diego flew off. Gretchen was resolute in her mind and believed that she owed it to Bertha and Colanda to be a support system and mother figure for Drake. She also believed that he was determined to lead a successful life and had already demonstrated a genuine need to belong.

Monday, October 22, was the beginning of Gretchen's final week before the variety show. She had gotten used to her routine walk every Monday for the past eight weeks, going along the whitewashed concrete corridor leading to the center's administrative office. The beautiful array of flowers lining both sides were breathtaking. The variations of red, yellow, orange, purple, and white dahlias reminded her of the flower garden she had loved as a child. She couldn't help noticing the freshly manicured and irrigated lawn and acres of maple, birch, and oak trees around her.

She entered the automatic sliding door and could see that the lobby was crowded that day. Almost all the chairs were occupied, and several people waited in line for the receptionist. She could see Martha, Trent's secretary, behind the brown wooden desk. Her royal-blue dress complimented her shoulder-length, curly red hair, Gretchen thought. She decided to take a stroll outside. A good time to get more acquainted with the surroundings, she was thinking, when she heard her name.

"Hi, Gretchen, please don't leave," Martha called out. "Trent will be here in five minutes."

"Thanks, Martha," Gretchen said. "I'll be in the faculty lounge until about noon. Please text me when he's available."

She walked to the end of the glossy terrazzo tile floor of the lobby. She entered a door to her right, and halfway down the carpeted hallway, she entered the faculty lounge, thinking as she went along, *I must put this matter to rest today.*

About three minutes later, while she sat at her desk, she was approached by Trent.

"Hi, Gretchen," he said. "I am so sorry to keep you waiting again. I see you are busy now. I'll be in my office. Feel free to walk right in when you are ready. I have about thirty minutes before my next meeting."

"Thanks for the consideration," she said. "I'll be there in five minutes."

Gretchen had decided to sit at her desk and take care of some admin duties while she waited. She picked up her black handbag from the desktop, and on her way out, she stopped by the round center table to look at some new pictures of faculty members. Her heart skipped a beat when she noticed one of Theo, dressed in his gray sweat suit with white sneakers. Gretchen picked up the picture and stared at it, wondering how it got there.

She returned the picture to its spot on the table and quickly exited the door.

She did not want to miss what she considered a critical meeting with Trent. Gretchen was thinking as she walked out of the lounge, *I'm hoping that Trent can explain his comment about cultural difference before the variety show tomorrow.*

She found him sitting at his desk and speaking on the phone. She was about to step back out and was surprised when he stopped her and said, "Please stay. I'm just about wrapping up this call. I've got to go now, Skip. I'll talk with you later."

He hung up the phone while beckoning to Gretchen to have a seat.

"Thanks for coming, and again, I apologize for my lateness.

I realized that we had postponed this meeting a few times before. Everyone's been so busy, with so much going on in the past four weeks."

"I understand. Thanks for finding time for me," she replied while making herself comfortable.

"Looking lovely as usual, Gretchen. How may I help you?"

Gretchen thanked him for the compliment. She was wearing a red cowl-neck sweater, slacks, and black loafers. She had felt a little uneasy by the way he was staring at her, but she managed to stay focused.

"I have three concerns," she began, "and I'll try to be quick."

"Take your time," Trent remarked.

"First, thanks for allowing me to work here. I am very appreciative of the confidence you have, that the students will be successful with me as their English literature instructor.

"Second, I'd rather I didn't answer to Skip if I continue working here. I am grateful that he got me this job, but his inappropriate behavior is troubling.

"Third, I need an explanation about the cultural differences you've stated as the reason why I won't play a lead role in the variety show."

Gretchen could hear her heart pounding in fear that she would be punished for speaking out.

"I didn't see this coming, and I'm very surprised," Trent said. "I'll do my best to satisfy you with my response. First, I must say that the students' overall performances so far have confirmed the success I expected. I thank you. Second, Skip is on the center's board of directors, but he is not the final authority on decisions I make. I want you to be the master of ceremonies, and cultural differences have never been a concern for me. Does that answer your concerns?"

"Yes, you did, thank you."

"I am a very good judge of character, and I don't fire people on a whim. That is an abuse of power and the worst form of discrimination, if the person is a minority. The teachers I hire usually stay, except the instructor you replaced. She couldn't handle this generation of students.

"I realized that the students had opened up with you on your first day and wanted to talk about racism. It was an eye-opener for me, and I'm glad that you initiated a platform for ongoing discussion on racism at the center, despite the potential for backlash. I will not walk away from this and allow the students, parents, and others to believe I don't care."

"Please know that I'm not here simply to be in the spotlight," Gretchen said. "I just want to support the center's mission."

"I believe that about you wholeheartedly, and I am here to ensure that you'll accomplish our mission. Don't worry."

Gretchen took the microtape from her purse and gave it to Trent. She could see him examining it with a puzzled look on his face.

"I found this on the lawn outside, the first day I met with you for the interview. I listened to it because I needed to track the owner, who happens to be your director."

Gretchen was satisfied when Trent said he would follow up with Skip about the tape. She let him know that she had kept a copy of the tape herself. As she exited the office, Trent had a troubled look on his face. Suffice it to say, Gretchen left his office feeling reassured.

Chapter 10

In the early morning of October 28, the day of the variety show, Gretchen sat journaling. She could hear her heart pounding and her tears flowed as sad memories of the devastating events kept flooding her mind. She had dreamed about this day but never realized it would be so nerve-racking, going against all odds to fulfill the Creator's plan. The previous day, the students finished their final rehearsal. She had a moment to spare before the event and decided to spend it journaling.

As part of the lesson plan for the semester, Gretchen had decided to complete the project planned by a previous instructor. The students were tasked to perform a scene from the play, *Merchant of Vanityville: The Verdict*. This would be their contribution to the fundraiser for the center.

Later that day, Gretchen reviewed the casting assignments with her students and ensured that everyone was prepared. At 6:30, Gretchen heard a resounding applause from the audience and joined in the clapping when she noticed Trent appear on the stage. The clapping stopped as he approached the podium and took up the microphone to speak. Gretchen realized in that moment that she still felt ambivalent about working at the center.

"Good evening," he began. "Thank you all and welcome. You are looking quite elegant yourselves. I am so proud to be headmaster of this fine institution, and I must say that I owe my success to you all. Throughout the five years I've been here, our dedicated Parent-Teachers Association and student body have rallied in support of our mission: To educate, nurture, and empower young minds."

Gretchen felt more confident as she joined in another round of applause. She noticed that Trent's eyes were on her as he continued to speak.

"Thank you, and I believe that this day will go down in history as a very memorable day. This year's variety show is a concerted effort, designed to bring our community members closer together. I was informed that this is the largest gathering ever hosted by us, capping at about eight hundred people. This is amazing! A special thanks to Dr. Mocktruman. Please join me on the stage, Gretchen."

Gretchen got out of her seat in the front row and walked briskly up the steps to join Trent at the podium. She looked pleasingly elegant in a vintage red/gold, long-sleeve Rococo gown and outshone Trent, standing beside her in his tuxedo outfit.

"Gretchen has gone above and beyond to have the students prepared for this occasion; they worked about eight weeks on this show. I will now turn over the rest of the night's program to Gretchen and her team."

Trent turned to her and said, "Tonight's performance is in your hands. Good luck."

Gretchen smiled and thanked him, while her eyes wandered around the theater, noticing the beautiful array of colors and elegance in the audience. Suddenly, her eyes met Skip's—piercing eyes, staring at her from the back row, center aisle, seat closest the door. Gretchen noticed that he was wearing a red shirt and black jacket. She could feel her heart pounding in her chest. She took a deep breath and looked to her left where Theo was seated in the front row. She could see him smiling at her and she smiled back.

Gretchen took the microphone and waited for the applause to stop. Then she said, "Good evening, everyone, and thank you very much for coming here to celebrate with us. I am also very happy to be here in this magnificent learning environment with your children, and I am honored to be among such a splendid group of people. It's my pleasure to declare the stage officially opened for our 2017 Variety Show. Relax and enjoy the performances of our budding young artistes as they present to you *Prelude to the Verdict*."

Gretchen could hear the resounding applause as she disappeared backstage, where she would spend most of her time assisting the performers. She could see and hear everything on a monitor. The curtains opened to reveal the Take Five Step band members in their black and gold tuxedos, doing their tap dance routine. Then Tapper Pepe and Company appeared on stage, in colorful matching outfits, tapped to "Happy." Gretchen couldn't help lip-syncing the words, shaking her head, and jigging to the words:

> Clap along if you feel like a room without a roof.
> Because I'm happy.
> Bring me down, can't nuthin'
> (happy, happy, happy)
> bring me down
> because I'm happy.

Gretchen's heart was aglow, reflected by a radiant smile on her face and a twinkle in her eyes as Theo appeared on stage. She watched as he performed the first song, a remake of "A Wonderland by Night," followed by "African Beats"—on his trumpet. He was backed by the Vanityville Concert Orchestra. Gretchen thought about the happy moment when Theo called for help and saved Bertha's life. Then the sad moment when they heard that Bertha had disappeared.

Gretchen quickly snapped back to the variety show when she heard the Vanityville Idol Quartet, in satin jade gowns with black lace tops, singing "Mr. Sandman." It made her remember the Chordettes' 1958 version. She began singing along with the quartet:

> Mr. Sandman, bring me a dream.
> Make him the cutest that I've ever seen.
> Give him two lips like roses and clover.
> Then tell him that his lonesome nights are over.

Gretchen was so pleased to hear such maturity and perfection in the four girls who were singing. She could see that older audience members enjoying the trip down memory lane with that song.

> So, please turn on your magic beam.
> Mr. Sandman, bring us, please, please, please,
> Mr. Sandman, bring us a dream.

Gretchen was truly impressed by Miwa, who played a piano solo by Beethoven. Gretchen was happy to see her mother enjoying the moment. Miwa was wearing a lovely pink lace gown and gold slippers.

Gretchen was aroused by the clapping at the end, which was followed by a brief silence. Then Meemee sang a jazz version of "How Glad I Am." She listened and watched with great admiration for Meemee, looking so beautiful in an elegant champagne gown with lace lantern sleeves, accessorized in gold. Gretchen was overtaken by grief when she heard the lines that reminded her of Bertha. She could not hold back the tears and wandered off in thoughts of Bertha writing.

> I wish I were a poet
> so I could express
> what I,
> what I'd like to say.
> I wish I were an artist

so I could paint a picture
of how I feel.
Oh, how I feel today.

Gretchen wiped away the tear and nodded in agreement with the words of Meemee's wonderful melody:

"My love has no walls on either side.
That makes my love wider than wide."

"And you don't know how glad I am," Gretchen said to herself as she continued listening to the music in the background and Meemee singing the last lines:

How glad I am.
How glad I am.

Then after the applause again, Nate walked onto the stage, with the assist of a cane, and joined Meemee. They reminded her of the gospel singers Sandi and Ron Patty, singing "It Took a Miracle" and "How I Love Him."

It took a miracle of love and grace.
O how I love him! How I adore Him!
My breath, my sunshine, my all in all!
This Great Creator became my Savior,
and all God's fulness dwelleth in Him.

They were simply wonderful, Gretchen thought as she cheered along with the audience.

The curtains opened for the play to begin. Katandria, in a black gown, walked onto the stage and began speaking.

> NARRATOR. Though the night be as black as death and fiend angelic hearts knew no mercy, love did find a way. In the Merchant of Vanityville, where fair is foul, and foul is fair, we gather to hear the *Verdict*.

> BAILIFF. *Hercules in a sheriff's uniform.* All rise. The Court of the Honorable Judge of Vanityville is now in session.

> JUDGE. *Annabella in a black robe with white cape.* Be seated. Sir Sleuthfoot, I have read your claim. This court will make a final judgment today. Is there anything else you would like to say?

> SLEUTHFOOT. *Patrick with long gray hair and beard, dressed in black shirt and red pantsuit.* I have been kind enough to loan money to this penniless woman in her times of need. Know that if this court denies my claim, surely misfortune will befall its statutes.

> JUDGE. Sir Sleuthfoot, you shall not be granted mercy being merciless. Counsel, is there anything else you will like to say?

> DANIELLE. Yes, Your Honor, if I may address the plaintiff's claim. I agree that no one should be forced to show mercy. Instead, mercy should be freely given, like the gentle rain that falls from heaven.

SLEUTHFOOT. You are starting to make sense, like a Danielle-come-to-justice. Solicitor, let me have my bond. (*To Madam Antoinette*: *Shenee, dressed in a black pantsuit.*) You unwise, ambitious borrower shall wear orange.

DANIELLE. Sir Sleuthfoot, keep your anxiety in check for a moment, in the same way you have held mercy captive. I am reading from the scroll in which the disclaimer states that any grudge or malice toward a borrower is deemed conflict of interest and grounds to make void or nullify a contract or agreement and any forfeiture therein. Did your bond state that provision in accordance with the law of Vanityville?

SLEUTHFOOT. I'll take the offer of twenty million dollars, offered at a previous hearing.

DANIELLE. Too late for change of a heart, and the question is not about the offer. Sir Sleuthfoot, can you prove to this court that it was your intent to enter into this contract agreement without malice toward Madam Antoinette? If you did verbally caution her, why did you not include your warning in your contract, to validate your intent?

SLEUTHFOOT. She should not be in business, if she did not know how to conduct herself the same way a businessman would.

DANIELLE. Would you treat me so cruelly were I in business with you?

SLEUTHFOOT. Perhaps not, for you would know better.

DANIELLE. If you would not treat me so cruelly, why did you treat Madam Antoinette so cruelly?

SLEUTHFOOT. I have done no wrong, and I do not have to show mercy for this penniless person whose failure should not go unpunished. Be reminded that there are institutionalized slave owners among you, Christians included, who treat certain workers as though they were cursed aliens. Yet I do agree that those slaves would be treated worse where they came from, and I should mind my own business.

DANIELLE. Sir Sleuthfoot, you make it my business when the victim is exploited and denied basic human rights such as the right to freedom from discrimination and the right to life, liberty, and personal security.

SLEUTHFOOT. Once again, if this is about mercy, and you must have your way, I'll take the previous offer of twenty million dollars.

DANIELLE. Sir Sleuthfoot, I'm not through with you yet. (*Addressing the judge.*) Your Honor, may it please the court that the precedent set in the case on *Shylock vs. Antonio* be applied in this case. I beseech the court to decree that upon Sir Sleuthfoot's death, part his estate will go to Madam Antoinette or her surviving children for all the suffering they had to endure, perpetually. I rest my case.

JUDGE. The court rules that Sir Sleuthfoot shall sign a bond with the terms as stated by Madam Antoinette, and his refusal to do so shall result in permanent confinement in Vanityville's penitentiary. Is that clear, Sir Sleuthfoot?

SLEUTHFOOT. It is very clear. Now grant me leave from your presence.

JUDGE. Sir Sleuthfoot, as soon as the agreement is signed, you may retreat to your place of abode until further notice. This court is dismissed.

At the end of the play, while the members of the cast were being introduced on stage, Gretchen decided to remove her costume as Danielle. To her surprise, the applause was resounding.

Gretchen listened as Trent said, "Ladies and gentlemen, boys and girls, please put your hands together for Gretchen Mocktruman, who played Danielle, the defense attorney."

The audience began clapping, whistling, and shouting, "Gretchen, we love you!"

Her attention was drawn to Sid in the audience. She recalled his remark (the night she went to Chuck's Place) that he hoped her English was as good as her looks. Gretchen watched him give her two thumbs up and smiled. She felt happy that the mission was accomplished.

The curtains closed for a ten-minute break. Gretchen retreated backstage. Her heart was joyful when she saw Theo approaching.

He gave thumbs up to the center's band members, preparing for their final song and dance.

Gretchen reappeared on stage. She was wearing Bertha's purple dress and black shoes. She walked to the center of the stage and announced, "Please stand with me for one minute of silence in honor of Bertha, an African American poet who had dedicated her life in service to this center."

Gretchen was pleased by the response. She could see everyone standing in silence, except Skip, sitting in the back row. She couldn't help noticing Skip speaking on his cell phone as he left the theater.

A minute later, as the audience sat, she declared, "Bertha, this one's for you," and while the orchestra played in the background, Gretchen poured out her heart into a song she wrote.

> My faith in God has taught me to stand
> when no one would dare stand with me.
> By His precious love
> and for His glory
> I shall stand.
> When the darts keep coming
> and all strength is gone,
> with no one to trust, to stand by me.
> But by His grace
> and for His glory, I shall stand.
> For His glory I shall stand.
> For His glory I shall stand.
> For His glory,
> For His glory I shall stand.

Gretchen felt overjoyed when she was joined by the Gentry Voices, singing "The Impossible Dream." The large group of performers did an amazing tribute to Bertha. Then Nate,

Meemee, and Theo joined the cast on stage, and Gretchen could hear their melodious voices sing the following lines:

> This is my quest:
> to follow the star.
> No matter how hopeless,
> no matter how far.
> To fight for the right
> without question or pause.
> To be willing to march into hell
> for a heavenly cause.

Gretchen's voice rang out with fervor and passion; looking up and pointing toward the sky, she continued to sing her heart out to the audience:

> And I know if I only be true to this glorious quest
> that my heart will lie peaceful and calm
> when I lay to my rest.

Gentry Voices joined Gretchen again, singing:

> To fight the unfightable foe,
> to reach the unreachable star.

Gentry Voices rang out in glorious harmony:

> To dream the impossible dream.

Gretchen noticed that Skip was back in his seat again, this time staring at her so much she could hear her heart pounding again. Instead of fear, she felt defiance, and Gentry Voices behind her bolstered her strength.

Gretchen was feeling reassured as she disappeared behind the purple curtains.

Another performer read a dramatic monolog entitled *For Slavery and a Pauper's Grave, I Thank You*, written by Gretchen's alter ego:

> Oh Creator, I thank you for blessings,
> small and great,
> for bittersweet memories, in sickness and in health
> I thank you for the will to love and not to hate,
> for bittersweet memories,
> in poverty and in wealth.
> But most of all,
> for overcoming slavery and a pauper's grave,
> I thank you.

Gretchen could not hold back the tears when she heard the Gentry Voices read another dramatic monolog:

> Bertha, the embodiment of Phillis,
> our beloved poet,
> you never ceased to love, to serve mankind,
> to glorify God.
> For the Creator's infinite wisdom was in you yet,
> unnoticed!
> Bertha, the embodiment of Phillis,
> our beloved poet,
> you never ceased to shine, to value mankind,
> to glorify God.
> They wanted a servant-slave and got a gifted poet.
> Yet, unnoticed!

Gretchen could hear the orchestra playing "Mission Impossible" and watched the slideshow as highlights played back scenes of the play. She saw her character, Danielle, pleading with Sleuthfoot to show mercy, Antoinette looking sorrowful, the honorable judge pleading with Sleuthfoot, who defended his forfeiture at the expense of mercy. The honorable judge lowered the gavel and delivered the verdict. Danielle ripped off her mask to reveal Gretchen; the audience applauding her.

Suddenly, Gretchen noticed that all the lights in the auditorium had gone out and the music had stopped. She could hear the audience shouting, "More, more," as they clapped and whistled.

"Please remain in your seats until your way is clear," Gretchen shouted. She clicked on the flashlight in her cellphone. The audience picked up on her cue and to her surprise the auditorium had enough lighting to keep the audience calm a bit. Gretchen found her way to the piano and started playing the song "You'll Never Walk Alone." She sang:

> When you walk through the storm,
> hold your head up high,
> and don't be afraid of the dark.
> At the end of the storm is a golden sky,
> and the sweet silver song of the lark.

Ding.

Gretchen noticed the word TRENT on her cell phone screen and quickly read his text while he played.

"Gretchen, I'm sure everyone is upset about the power outage. This must be an awkward moment for you, I'll be there shortly to give the closing remark. Thanks for trying to keep the audience entertained. You're awesome."

Gretchen voice texted back:

"I appreciate your input. Thank you too."

Within seconds, she was watching Trent on stage and heard his closing remarks.

"On behalf of Dr. Gretchen Mocktruman and her team of performers, I apologize for the power outage, although it came close to the end of the show. A tragic accident at Marshvalley Creek bridge may have caused it. I take this opportunity to thank you all for coming. You have made this momentous occasion possible and amid the unhappy ending, life must go on. Those of you who will be traveling north, try to avoid the bridge, if you can. Good night and be safe."

Gretchen continued playing the piano, softly and watched as individuals in the audience gave hugs and kisses and slowly dispersed. She was very surprised but felt uplifted at the same time when she noticed the Gentry Voices return to the stage. They stood behind her with their cell lights on. She could see Trent looking amazed as he listened to the harmonious voices. He smiled in admiration and clapped with the remaining audience as they paused to listen.

> Walk on, through the wind.
> Walk on, through the rain.
> Though your dreams be tossed and blown.
> Walk on, walk on, with hope in your heart,
> and you'll never walk alone.
> You'll never walk alone.

Gretchen could hear the audience clapping as they exited. She walked over to her wonderful students and hugged each one of them. The moment felt surreal to Gretchen. *There couldn't have been a happier ending*, she thought.

Later, Gretchen learned that the local police had received a call from someone who reported that a strange woman, dressed in purple and barefooted, was lurking around the neighborhood. She was last seen on the bridge near Coventry Landing and Marshvalley Creek and appeared to be dangerous. The police tracked the caller to a black Lexus owned by Skip Crotalus. A police chase ensued and ended minutes later when the Lexus ran into the bridge. The car landed in the creek, in the exact spot where Bertha's white car crashed over two months ago. A positive identification revealed that the driver of the Lexus was Skip. The car was thoroughly searched, and no evidence of foul play found. No eyewitness has come forth, and a thorough investigation is under way.

Gretchen experienced an array of emotions when she got the news. Despite feeling numb, she managed to smile a little, feeling very proud about the students' outstanding performances. She was saddened by the news about Skip's tragic accident but relieved that the media could give an account of what had happened. She felt a sense of closure, unlike with Bertha's accident and disappearance.

The following Friday afternoon was Gretchen's final class with the students. She could hear the laughter and was pleased to recognize the harmony among the students as they talked about the variety show and what they've learned in English lit. Gretchen was sitting at her desk, watching and listening.

"Mine is the simile in 'the night be as black as death.' I love it," said Malcom.

"Fiend angelic hearts knew no mercy," Gretchen heard someone shout from the back.

"Oxymoron," another student shouted back.

"My favorite figure of speech used in the Merchant of Vanityville is the metaphor 'held mercy captive,'" said Shenee.

Gretchen could hear her apologize for not feeling well to perform in the role of 'Danielle'. "I'm so glad Miss Gretchen could fill in for me, and she nailed it," said Shenee.

"I won't forget the paradox in 'fair is foul, Sleuthfoot,' and 'foul is fair, Danielle.' That's my favorite, and Miss Gretchen, as Danielle, is my hero," Katandria declared as she smiled at Gretchen, and the other students applauded with her.

Gretchen smiled back and was very grateful.

"'Bertha, the embodiment of Phillis our beloved poet' is a good example of personification," said Annabelle.

"I didn't understand that part. Who is Phillis?" Miwa asked.

"Didn't you see her in the purple dress?" asked Annabella.

"My mom has everything on tape," Miwa said. "I'll watch it again later."

"I didn't like having to play Sleuthfoot's role, but I'm sure I did make him a proud loser," Patrick said, and everyone including Gretchen had a good laugh. They hugged, cried, and said their goodbyes.

Later in Trent's office, as she said goodbye, Gretchen was so happy to hear Trent's report.

"For the first time in my five years here at the center, I've seen everyone feeling happy. They all passed, with many getting As and no one lower than a C."

Chapter 11

Eight laps in eleven minutes, not bad, Gretchen thought to herself, panting as she came to a halt. The sconces around the outer edge of the track provided the lighting she needed as it was still a little dark. Four more laps, and she'd complete her mile-and-a-half run, which she planned to accomplish next time.

"It is Sunday, October 21, 2018," she typed into her cell. "What should have been two weeks with Theo has turned out to be more than two months already. I am having a wonderful time in Vanityville. We visited Nate and his family and took many trips around Gentry Cove. I became very involved with Theo's research. I found his topic about disenfranchised youths very fascinating. I got to visit Dunkersfield again, the marshlands this time, which seemed very familiar to where I visited Bertha when she was caring for Ed and Lizzy. I understand why it is called no-man's land."

Gretchen was about to type another thought into her cell when Theo's voice interrupted her:

"Up early, as usual. Who are you texting at five thirty in the morning?"

She turned to the direction of the voice and noticed Theo approaching from behind, to the left of her.

"Myself, before I forgot. Sneaking up on me?" she retorted.

"Not at all. I was out here an hour ago," Theo said.

"I didn't see you. Why were you up so early?"

"I couldn't sleep and needed to clear my head. My recliner on the patio is my little sanctuary. Besides, I have a few errands to run today and will be leaving soon."

Gretchen put the cell phone in the pouch around her waist and pulled her white T-shirt over her black tights. Then she reached for Theo's hand and invited him to sit on the bench with her.

"It's been such a struggle lately for me to keep up with my Tabata training, but this past week has been a time of healing for me. Thanks to you, Theo."

"Didn't mean to get in your way. Do you need some privacy to finish typing your thoughts?"

"That can wait. I didn't mean to sound impolite; I didn't really think you were snooping."

"No need to apologize. I understand."

"Theo, you are never in my way but always in my thoughts. You're my strong tower, one in a million, and I'll forever be grateful."

"I am very happy to know that, and I enjoyed watching those feet of yours run. I watched all eight of the laps and can imagine you competing. You must come from a line of athletic people. Were you a star athlete in your younger days?"

"Yes, I was a well-recognized athlete in my high school years and could have gone to college on track scholarship, except I was more academically inclined. Books have been my all-time favorite companion and writing, my most popular pastime."

"You're quite a phenomenal woman."

He noticed the number 11 printed on the back of her shirt.

"My favorite number is eleven," he remarked.

"Interesting! I am just finishing up chapter 11 of my manuscript and decided to dedicate it to you."

"I wanted to avoid asking questions, but am I getting in your way?"

"No, you're not. I would've let you know. Openness is another trait we have in common. Is it about my manuscript?"

"Partially."

"What is it?"

"Well …." Theo hesitated and then continued, "Things your manuscript didn't or couldn't mention.

"I understand the couldn't part, but what didn't I mention that I should have?"

"It would be unfair to your book if I were to list what it didn't mention."

"So do you think it is perfect?"

"I must say that I could feel your passion and hear your cry for deliverance from evil. Your manuscript is relevant; it's rich and well-written, but there are a few holes."

"One that's been haunting me for the past week, now that I am here, is my need to know who broke into your house and why."

"I'm not sure of the answer, but I'm not too worried about it. I am a Vietnam veteran and have not forgotten my craft."

"I believe you, but I can't let this one rest. Someone must have known you'd be out of town on August 13 when you came to visit me in Dunkersfield and consider the timing; it must have been between 6:00 and 7:45, the time you left, and the time Nate arrived to find your home burglarized. Someone must be in close range to your home and watching your every move."

"Gretchen, I'm also a practicing psychologist and very good at math, but I don't have the gift for detective work."

"That's all you need: a little knowledge in psychology and math to figure things out."

Gretchen noticed that Theo was smiling at her comment, and it got her even more worked up.

"You are also a combat angel, and if I, being a mortal soul, can follow you in my dreams and know your thoughts, why is it difficult for you to do detective work?"

"Come here."

Gretchen could feel Theo holding her close; it was such an intense moment to her because she had felt the need for his touch so badly. He could feel her yearning, but he had to stay focused.

"Gretchen, I'll be whatever you want me to be. Which way should I wiggle, baby?"

"Punkey, is that you?"

"Who is Punkey?"

"My deceased husband who had said those words to me before. He was portrayed as my worm and I like a saint."

"A worm can become a butterfly," Theo said as he tried to muddle her mind.

Gretchen kept him drifting along in her response. "A butterfly can become an angel."

After a brief pause, a contemplative Theo replied, "Do you have a trilogy in mind?"

"If it pleases the Creator. There are so many gaps to fill, one book would be a never-ending story."

"And I would certainly love to meet Punkey after we round up the children."

Gretchen looked up into Theo's face as she whispered, "Sometimes I want to believe that you are Punkey in a white man's skin, and I know that all things are possible with the Creator. You remind me of Punkey in so many ways. He died and left me a widow in 1993, one year before I met Phillis. He was also a Vietnam veteran, and sometimes you say things I've heard him say in the vernacular. I see many similar traits: very loving, witty, protective, spiritual and discerning."

"Do you still love him?"

"Very much, I do."

"I can identify with that feeling. I know exactly where you are coming from."

Gretchen could see the twinkle in Theo's eyes and the tears welled up in them.

"I am waiting in purgatory—being purified—to get my wings, but I'll return to earth, if that's what it will take. I cannot watch you get hurt anymore."

She continued to believe that she was talking to Theo.

"I know dreams can be weird sometimes, but I don't need you to go back there. I will. All I need is for you to help me wrap up this case, for Bertha's sake. It's been going on for too long."

"I agree. You've completed a tremendous amount of work already but will need a little help with your manuscript."

"Some gaps will be bridged once we find Bertha and maybe other innocent souls who have disappeared and bring Butch and company to justice."

"And things will get worse unless we act quickly," Theo said.

"That's what I'm talking about," she said.

In their minds, they agreed that once a picture was painted, it becomes real, but "reality" is always questionable and may never be known.

Gretchen had started to accept the belief that her escape from reality was inevitable. The void and loneliness that existed in her life could go away only in dream world. She felt that her existence mattered or had any value only when she was in Theo's world.

"My precious and blessed Li'l Pearl, I love you. Please don't worry."

Gretchen closed her eyes, took a deep breath, and exhaled slowly as Theo's words reverberated in her head.

My precious and blessed Li'l Pearl, I love you.

"This is your chapter, so revel in it," she replied.

"If I didn't know you well enough, I would say you are very playful, but not in a childish way."

"Theo, I can't wait for this nightmare to be over, so I can go back to my normal self again."

"Didn't I call you a saint before?"

"It was many years ago, but I remember, and I'm glad that you enlightened me. However, I'd like to stay with Theo and enjoy this trip with him, if you don't mind."

Gretchen realized that it was not her comfort zone, but she was easily adaptable, another rare quality Theo had noticed about her.

"I'll never get tired listening to you."

"But we must eat."

"What would you like?"

Theo offered to prepare breakfast while Gretchen freshened up, and he suggested that they discuss her manuscript, the ten chapters he'd reviewed so far.

"I could do both."

"No, not this time."

Gretchen realized that Theo was bent on fixing breakfast as he took her hand and led back toward the patio. Gretchen could see the L-shaped patio and felt the radiant energy from the sun rising in the east as they walked.

"You've fed me for a whole week," Theo said, "so it's my turn to feed you. We'll talk more about the main characters over breakfast."

"Sounds like a good plan, my super chef. I'm in," Gretchen said as she received a smooch from Theo and was on her way.

"Any food allergies?" Theo asked.

"None," she called back and could feel his eyes on her as she scampered up the stairs.

Inside the kitchen, Theo felt like a pro whisking up three egg yolks, lemon juice, salt, and red pepper in a glass bowl, making a creamy yellow hollandaise sauce. Then he noticed the water boiling in the saucepan on the stovetop.

"Time to poach a couple eggs, two sets," he said as if he knew someone was watching.

Meanwhile, Gretchen was in the guest bedroom above, her favorite place in Theo's house. She was in deep contemplation while getting dressed.

"It's been very difficult for me, trying to erase Skip from my memory, although I'm aware that there can be no real peace until evil is eradicated," she told herself.

As she brushed her hair into a ponytail, her attention was drawn to the fuchsia chiffon curtains. They were being swayed by a mild wind blowing through the window. She noticed further that the window was opened.

She was sitting on the white vanity stool, applying a touch of lipstick, when she got a text from Theo:

"I summon you to the back patio, where breakfast is served."

She texted back, "I'll be down in a minute."

Theo has made me feel very much at home here, she thought. *I'll be sad when it's time for me to go.*

As she brushed off the loose strands of hair from her fuchsia T-shirt, Gretchen could also see the angel on the back and thought she looked well put together in her blue jeans and black loafers. She hurried over to the open window and closed it. Then she exited the side door and went down the stairs.

Gretchen was surprised to see how fast Theo had breakfast ready. He pulled out a chair for her to sit at the small coffee table set for two. She quickly noticed the eggs Benedict, topped with Hollandaise sauce and chives on her plate. She also noticed two glasses, one with milk, the other with water, and a bowl of fresh fruit as well.

"Mouth-watering. The way to start a day. Thank you," Gretchen said while Theo got himself comfortable in the chair opposite her, his back to the patio rail.

"My pleasure."

She reached for his left hand and squeezed it gently; he closed his eyes as he listened.

"For what we are about to receive, we give thanks," she prayed.

Theo could feel her release his hand, and he opened his eyes, staring into hers.

"Gretchen, I would say you are a breath of fresh air, if I didn't know the taste of vintage wine. So close to perfection, my sweet lady in fuchsia, you perk my appetite. Let's eat."

"The feeling is mutual. Thank you."

They smiled and kept looking at each other as she ate her eggs and he munched on a slice of apple from his fruit bowl.

"Let's talk about *Resurrected Gentry Crossing Over,*" Theo said.

"What other gaps did you discover?" she asked, eager to know.

"I would put your manuscript among the Creator's masterpieces. It is truly a magnificent work of a genius," she heard him say. "Gretchen, correct me if I am wrong. You started writing this manuscript in 2005 but had to set it aside because of postgraduate studies and other critical challenges in your life. Then you resumed writing in 2010, when it struck you that your destiny was starting to resemble that of Bertha's. In your mind, she is the spiritual embodiment of Phillis Wheatley, the African American poet you became fascinated by in 1994. Phillis was enslaved, mistreated, and her life ended in a pauper's grave, 234 years ago, when she was about thirty years old.

"After many excellent accomplishments, your life became ravaged by chronic unemployment and one misfortune after another. You became fearful that a pauper's grave would be your fate as your life spiraled downward. You sought refuge in dreamland Vanityville, Gentry Cove, where you found Bertha and bumped into me, Theo, your guardian angel, and Skip, your nemesis. Your experiences with them have confirmed that love, like hate, can be eternal.

"Finally, you began to heed Bertha's voice, telling you to write, and you are convinced that it is the Creator's perfect will that you finish this story. One year and nine months after Bertha's disappearance, you are still hoping to find closure in *Resurrected Gentry, Crossing Over,* the story designed to redeem the Bertha— Phillis embodiment from a pauper's grave."

"I couldn't have summed up those ten huge chapters any better," said Gretchen.

"Where should I begin my critique?" Theo asked.

"Please start with Colanda, if you don't mind. Her death and disappearance might bring us closer to Bertha, her mother and my spiritual sister in grief."

"I agree. Though a peripheral character, Colanda's demise was a heart-wrenching, soul-searching moment for me. I didn't realize until now that being heavenly minded with little earthly good cannot earn me wings. I let Earl down big time. How could I have allowed the adversary to walk into his home and devastate his family, my family? I was blessed with the spirit of discernment, yet I couldn't see that she was in danger. I had distanced myself to where I couldn't hear her cry for help. I couldn't be the father figure in Drake's life. Worthless man that I am, I failed."

"Theo, please don't berate yourself like that. You did not know," Gretchen interjected.

"That's exactly the point. I should have known, and I did know that Colanda was a widow, and her son Drake, my nephew, was a fatherless child. That's all I needed to know to feel the need to protect them."

Gretchen was tearing up inside to see Theo in such agony and offered a suggestion: "Let's continue this discussion later."

"I must be held accountable. You've all heard her in her final hours, six years later, when her world was about to collapse, and I listened when it was too late. The serpent had already sunk its fangs in her and ensured that she took her last breath. All along, mental illness in a dysfunctional home with a disrespectful young adult were to blame: the scapegoats, while the perpetrator launched one attack after another. Then finally, an innocent life is gone, before I, the famous psychologist, started paying attention."

"Theo, please don't be so unkind to yourself. Colanda's death is a common occurrence among the disenfranchised. I'm sure you would've done more for her if you could. Besides, it's not over yet. Her demise may help us to bring redemption for others, including Bertha."

"Gretchen, I understand what you mean by demise, but we should not worry about those who were wrongly put to sleep eternally. Instead, we should mourn for those who have no hope[15] for salvation from the evil they harbor in their hearts. When the fullness of time has come, the grave shall give up the innocent.[16] Then, some of those who yet remain, shall be caught up to meet them in the clouds."[17]

"I have no doubt about that," Gretchen said.

"The Creator shall wipe away all tears," Theo said, "and though it seems that evil is prevailing, I am reassured that love shall surely endure."

Gretchen watched and listened, oblivious of everything else around her, as if in a trance, captivated by Theo's angelic and sweet-sounding voice.

"Love incarnate, so divine, overcame death on the cross. The story is riveted indelibly in my mind, as if it had happened only three days ago and not over two thousand years ago,"[18] Theo declared.

Theo admitted that he might've rejected the Creator's earthly existence in the form of His Son, because of skepticism and gross prejudice, the epitome of ignorance. He might've been one who stood quietly and watched Jesus suffer, when He was given thirty-nine lashes (He was spared the fortieth lash because it would be considered criminal).[19] He could've witnessed Him being given vinegar with gall.[20] He believed also that he might've been

---

[15] 1 Thessalonians 4:13.

[16] Daniel 12:2.

[17] Ecclesiastes 12:7.

[18] 2 Peter 3:8.

[19] 2 Corinthians 11:24.

[20] Matthew 27:34.

there when God's Son was falsely blamed, mocked and nailed to a wooden cross, the wreath of thorns being put around His head. Theo believed he might've stood there and watched it all from God's view, three days ago. He might've condoned the cruel crucifixion[21]—Christ's unjust reward for His impeccable integrity and excellence in service to humanity.

"I thank you for enlightening me," Gretchen said. "I might've been there too because I've come to identify with Christ's suffering. I'm glad that the Creator has sent me here."

"Gretchen, I am fully aware that Bertha-Phillis's redemption means a lot to you, and rightfully so, but don't be too hard on yourself. You, like many others, have suffered various forms of cruelty for the sake of being loyal to your faith and country."

Gretchen listened attentively as Theo said that she must be compensated for all the wrong done to her, for simply loving and doing the right things so that her world might be a better place. She agreed that suffering widows, fatherless children, and other disenfranchised individuals should not be predisposed to eternal doom. She was very happy when Theo shared that Drake had found his way out and had found true love in Daisy. He has been a loving father to Drake Jr. and was doing well in his job.

"I have no doubt that Colanda shall be in a happier place," Theo said, "and she's proud of Drake. Will the Creator who is rich in mercy[22] be silent forever and allow innocent souls to suffer eternally? Will planet earth be allowed to go into ruins because of evil when good is working hard to prevent it?"

"Again, it is your chapter," Gretchen said. "Revel in it. I could sit here and listen to you all day."

"I thank God every day for you, Nate, Meemee, my little grandson, Drake, and my immortal relatives. I can't wait to see the day when we shall all be reunited."

---

[21] John 19:1–39; Matthew 27:34–44.

[22] Ephesians 2:4.

"Could you handle all of us around you at the same time?"

"Hmm, good question. You know that my track record is not so good. I tend to give my undivided attention to one hurting soul at a time."

Gretchen watched as Theo walked around to her chair and took her by the hand. He invited her to walk with him to the family room. He walked over to the entertainment center, inserted a CD into the player, and led Gretchen to the open space between the fireplace and the center table.

Theo was in complete rapture when Gretchen's warm body collapsed in his arms. He could see the familiar sadness in her eyes, trying to overpower her beauty. She could see the look of love in his eyes and hear their hearts pounding. Then she broke the silence by telling him how she was feeling:

"Theo, sometimes I get the feeling that I may not see you again, and it scares me."

"Don't be afraid. If I never get to see you here, after today, I'll take it that you've gone home. Yet I don't believe that'll be for a while. We have work to do here, that you can't do there, but it's not for me to say."

Theo pulled Gretchen close to him again as they listened to the song playing in the background: "It's Not for Me to Say." They locked into a slow dance, Gretchen's head on his chest.

> "It's not for me to say
> you love me.
> It's not for me to say you'll always care."

Theo began singing along, Gretchen still clinging to him:

> "Oh, but here for this moment I can hold you fast
> and press your lips to mine
> and dream that love will last.
> As far as I can see,

this is heaven."

She turned her face up to his; they kissed, slowly, long. Then Theo started singing along again, looking into her eyes:

"Or we may never meet again.
But then,
it's not for me to say."
They danced.

He swept her off her feet and spun her around as she anchored her arms around his neck. She could tell he was very happy, and it made her feel very happy too. As he set her down on the sectional sofa and sat beside her, they could hear the buzzing on his cell phone. Gretchen saw a disappointed look on his face as he looked at his cell.

He noticed that the call was from Vanityville Police.

"I do need to take this," he said, apologizing.

"I understand," Gretchen remarked as she pulled up beside him and gently stroked his back in support. Theo listened for about thirty seconds and then said, "I'll be there in about five minutes."

He exhaled, feeling slightly frustrated as he explained to Gretchen, "I have to visit the station for a police lineup."

"You do need to go. Will five minutes be enough time to get there?"

"Yes, it's just across from the marina."

Gretchen watched, feeling a bit disappointed as Theo walked quickly toward the front door.

"Please promise me that you'll finish chapter 11 by the time I return."

"I promise," Gretchen said, smiling.

Chapter 12

Chapter 11 is done, as I promised, Gretchen thought as she threw herself into her comfy bed. And now, I am determined to write perhaps the final chapter. It's like giving birth: painfully sweet.

She was overjoyed so far, knowing that Theo had given positive feedback about her manuscript, and he genuinely had her best interest at heart. Gretchen had come to realize that Theo was very down-to-earth and practical. She could not believe her eyes when she saw a pink letter-size envelope addressed to her, from him. It was on the right end table, near her laptop. She quickly opened the envelope and removed the white parchment paper. She wiped away the tears welling up in her eyes, propped herself up in the bed, and read Theo's letter.

> Dear Gretchen,
>
> My precious and blessed Li'l Pearl, words cannot express how much I love you, but I'll try anyway.
>
> You have chosen me, and I thank you. Yet I have asked to be your guardian angel of St. Uriel, in conjunction with St. Raphael's Band. The Creator's fire and thunder, protector of women and children, shall work in unison with the angel of peace on your behalf. My mission is twofold,

involving you and Bertha, my final assignment
before I make wings. On the one hand, I get a
chance to love you, knowing it shall not return to
me void. On the other hand, you get to love me,
and for the same reason. You are the superlative
embodiment of love that's lacking in your world
today. For that reason, you are disliked by those
who despise your faith and God's gift of love in
you. I shall ensure justice and deliverance from
all evil. Everything that was taken from you
shall be restored tenfold. Your sufferings, selfless
humanitarian sacrifices, and unconditional love
shall not be in vain. Dr. Mocktruman, please
be assured, your cry has been heard, and the
Creator shall grant you the desires of your heart.
Resurrected Gentry Crossing Over is all over but
for the shouting.

Forever yours,
Theodorus

Gretchen felt very grateful for saving grace. The affirmations
she received from Theo were inspiring. The thought of having to
wake up in a place where she was not welcomed, had no hope for
self-efficacy, and was denied the basic amenities of life scared her.
She felt that it would be better to dwell in her dream world instead.
As she waited for Theo's return, and between reading, listening
to music, and meditating, she journaled.

Although journaling sometimes made Gretchen feel like she
was reopening wounds that were better left alone, because of the
potential for more pain, it was usually therapeutic. Documenting
the events made her feel like a burden was lifted and injustice was
repressed. Her explanation was that from a medical standpoint,
some wounds must be reopened intentionally. They needed to
be reexamined and treated, where necessary, to ensure healthy

wound closure and healing. She recalled Bertha's plea for nurses to intervene as voices for the voiceless and concurred that such an intervention was necessary, particularly where the call for mental health nursing was concerned. Not necessarily for victims but also for the oppressive bullies.

Gretchen also endorsed Bertha's concern about the division among nurses and the need for protection against discrimination and unfair treatment in the workplace. The problem was race-related, an intolerance of diversity. The underlying reason was that dreamers from certain socioeconomic and ethnic backgrounds should not aspire to be leaders or dictate to people in corporate societies in America. For instance, individuals like Gretchen and Bertha should only be slaves or settle for jobs that individuals with superior intellectual abilities did not want; this was the subtle and unwritten rule. They who'd felt it knew it.

Gretchen felt support for Bertha's determination to reclaim their professions and establish lines of demarcation. Honoring the dream and faith of America's Founding Fathers was Gretchen's and Bertha's heart cry. Why should a nurse or an educator or anyone be forced to settle for a lesser vocation? Or why should those who have given blood, sweat, and tears—their hearts and souls—for America, the beloved, not reap the benefits? Why should they be made to suffer gross unemployment, financial hardship, homelessness, and abject poverty? It wasn't their idea that education should be the key to success, but they got punished for being educated. Instead, they were labeled "overachievers" and forced home on sabbatical, indefinitely.

Gretchen and Bertha were ripped from the people they served and were at the mercy of others who felt empowered to prey on their vulnerability, knowing no one would come to their rescue. It was very painful to be treated with such disrespect, as if they lacked the competence or leadership skills. Moreover, after having had their skills authenticated, it was more than excruciating to be displaced from the workforce while watching others make a mockery of their professions. It wasn't that they wanted to be rich. They simply wanted to actualize their true potential and God-given gifts while serving others. This was their American dream, their pursuit of happiness, their inalienable right. Unlike those who avoided the dust of the arena, Gretchen and Bertha suffered and died to self and in unconditional love for country, for all people.

Gretchen also believed that journaling helped her to explain her movements between the realm of dream and real-time experiences, and the need to cohesively weave the parts together. The gaping crevices between dreamland–Vanityville, Gentry Cove, where she often escaped to, and the reality from which she was eager to escape, might seem philosophical expositions. Yet she wanted to be careful not to inflict more pain by rehashing events. Although separate realms, seemingly requiring separate books, this one story served the purpose of affirming the Creator's omnipresence, omniscience, and omnipotence. The ever-present, all-knowing, and all-powerful God watches over all of us, on whatever planet. Whither shall we flee from His presence?[23]

On October 22, 2018, when Gretchen opened her eyes, she could feel the familiar pat on her shoulders and noticed a purple-red angelic glow in her living room. She could see a figure standing at the foot of her mattress and heard these angelic words: "I will never leave you nor forsake you."

Gretchen believed it was Bertha. She was in full view, dressed in purple, with her wings folded. Her face was blurred, and within seconds, she disappeared. Gretchen was fully awake and began looking around the room. Her eyes became fixed on the portraits on the wall opposite her air mattress. She noticed the time on

---

[23] Psalm 139:7.

her cell phone: it was 4:05 a.m. A calm feeling came over her when she thought that Bertha had crossed over. Yet she was a bit disappointed that Theo left her at his house; she hadn't heard from him for more than twenty-four hours. She had felt reassured after he danced with her and gave her the most passionate kiss ever. It was heavenly. Yet when he said goodbye, it was as if her dream had ended.

She had awakened to find that the reality of the place she called home was only a vacant house. All her furniture had been put in storage more than two years ago, for which she owed hundreds of dollars in storage fees. The inflatable mattress, small table, two chairs, and TV remained the only household items in her possession.

Gretchen's tears were of mixed emotions. The first was sadness, knowing that she may be homeless soon. Simultaneously, her tears reflected happiness, knowing that Bertha was there. Her eyes wandered to the two portraits she intentionally kept on the wall. The one to the right was a nondescript appearance of herself in the purple dress. She was the slave-servant who loved unconditionally but never felt loved. The portrait on the left was her in the beautiful Elizabethan gown she wore to the variety show in Vanityville. Her radiance and elegance still shone through, a true portrait of the lady that she was. Those three words— integrity, service, excellence—engraved on the bottom panels of each picture frame defined the character traits in her and Bertha.

Bertha, she thought, *I would accommodate a pair of wings to fly away from here, since I don't drive, but you are in a more deserving position to be an angel.*

<hr>

The same evening, while Gretchen was asleep, she dreamed that she was walking with Theo, after having dinner at a popular restaurant near the marina. They were attacked in the parking lot by three men in hoods. It was too dark to see clearly, but she noticed that one was very tall, and the other two were shorter than her. In a split-second, the two men pounced on Theo, and the third, a short, heavyset figure, swiftly approached Gretchen. She could see him reaching for something in his jacket pocket, but she sprayed mace in his eyes. As the chemical took effect, Gretchen sprayed again. She couldn't stop to help the screaming attacker because she was busy distancing herself. She was about to dial 911 when she heard sirens wailing and noticed the police and ambulance had gathered.

She found out later that Theo had been stabbed in the shoulder. However, he had managed to disarm the assailant, who was tackled and restrained by a few bystanders until the police showed up. The short one was found with dislocated hips, but no one seemed to know how. Gretchen could see the familiar purple-red light fading as more people gathered. Then she woke up.

She was feeling sad and a little depressed, so much that she virtually cried herself back to sleep. It was one o'clock in the morning when Gretchen felt herself twitching and heard her groans getting louder. She was excited to see the purple glow, just the way Bertha would present. Gretchen was lying on her back and could see the curtains swaying, and a mild wind sent chills down her spine. Bertha was standing at the window opposite the bed. Gretchen noticed that the glow was fading, and Bertha's silhouette was more distinctive. Her wings opened and closed slowly. Then Gretchen realized that Bertha was trying to communicate with her. She could hear the words: "When in doubt and despair, think deeply."

So Gretchen started thinking deeply. She could sense that Bertha's glow had gotten brighter. Gretchen noticed the glow radiating toward the bedroom door to her right, and the knob was turning slowly. Then her attention was drawn back to Bertha, who she noticed was in full glow from head to feet, and her wings were wide open.

My heart is pounding, more in awe for Bertha's angelic presence than fear of an intruder, Gretchen thought. *I was prepared to fight to the last breath, but obviously Bertha seems to be in control of the situation.*

Gretchen could see a figure dressed in black enter the room. It was holding an object in its hand. Then she saw the figure make an about-face and bolt out the door.

Whoever it is did not expect to be greeted by an angel and obviously wasn't prepared for a confrontation with Colanda's angry black mother-angel, she thought.

By the time her feet hit the floor beside her bed, she heard a loud thud.

Perhaps the intruder crash-landed in the foyer downstairs, Gretchen mused.

She decided against calling 911 to avoid reporting that Bertha had scared an intruder from Theo's house. Besides, she did not want to disturb the peace in the neighborhood so early in the morning. Then she noticed that Bertha was gone. The window was closed, but she could see someone limping briskly toward a black van; she took a snapshot as the figure opened the door on the passenger side and jumped into the vehicle, which pulled away and headed north on South Cove Estate Drive. Gretchen closed her eyes and thought quickly.

I must report what has happened at some point, Gretchen thought, noticing it was 3:10 a.m.

There was nothing stirring. She could hear a pin drop and followed her gut feeling that it was safe for her to go downstairs. She could hear Bertha's voice saying, "Do not be afraid; angel Raphael[24] and others keep watch over you."

My Tuesday's angel of peace, Gretchen reminded herself as she quickly freshened up. Feeling reassured and calm, she proceeded cautiously down the stairs and went into the family

---

[24] Tobit 12:15; Revelation 8:2.

room. She flipped on the lights and quickly looked around. She took snapshots of the bloodstain on the floor below the loft. She recalled hearing the thud when the intruder was making good an escape. She texted Leo.

"Good morning, please pick me up in ten minutes at Coventry Landing."

I'll jog and meet him halfway, Gretchen thought.

She could feel Bertha's presence in the house. The purple-red glow was moving along with her. Then she heard her voice: "When you can't see, trust the Creator's lead."

Gretchen's mind was made up, and she prayed for wisdom and courage. She noticed that it was 3:30 a.m. on her cell phone when she picked up Theo's copy of the key to Colanda's house from the key rack in the kitchen. She made sure that her scissors and little penlight were in the pouch around her waist. She emptied her bladder, drank a few sips of water, and put a bottle in her pouch. Then she left a note.

"I'll be at Colanda's house; will return with key.

"Gretchen"

As she walked through front door, she noticed that lights were on in the bedroom window of Miwa's house across the street. She could see the silhouette of someone standing at the front window of the top floor and taking pictures. Gretchen felt a lightness about her as she ran. It was as if she was on the track again. It was very dark out, but the streetlights helped her to see. She ran as fast as she could along the jogging trail on South Cove Drive. In less than five minutes, she was at the junction with Coventry Landing. She could see the mound with the purple cornflowers around the base. Then she saw Leo in his silver Dodge, faithfully waiting for her.

Gretchen got in the car, and Leo took off. She gave him instructions as he drove. He turned left on Gentry Cove Highway, toward the marina, then left on Marshvalley Creek Circle to Colanda's house, the third on the left. She instructed Leo to park in the driveway and wait for her in the car. She walked up to the front door and opened it cautiously. She went inside and could tell that the house was empty.

This is strange, she thought as she recalled the pictures Theo had taken the day Colanda passed away. Before she could go up the stairs, she heard a scream and thought of Leo.

Then Gretchen heard Bertha's voice: "Think deeply."

So she closed her eyes and thought. Then she took out her cell phone and got a few snapshots of the empty house. Within seconds of returning her cell to the pouch and zipping up her dress, she heard footsteps and voices. She had just enough time to crouch out of the way in the little hollow behind the stairwell.

Gretchen could feel Bertha's presence in the house; her glow was the brightest she'd ever seen. The front door opened. She could hear the voices of two men conversing as they entered the house.

"Maybe that guy was an illegal alien trying to steal what's left of Colanda's stuff, but we beat him to the punch."

"But how did he get in?"

"I don't know. Maybe he was waiting for someone else to show up with a key. You know that Colanda's son is still around."

"Okay, let's go get the other body and get out of here."

Gretchen could hear the men's footsteps going upstairs and realized that they could not see Bertha's glow. She seized the opportunity to get into the black van, which was backed up close to the doorway. She could see the shape of a body tied in crocus bags and blood on the floor of the van, and she thought of Leo. It was difficult, but she remained calm as she hid behind some cardboard boxes in the corner of the van. Then Gretchen heard the men returning, and she kept still, barely breathing. She heard a thud as they threw what Gretchen thought to be another body into the van. She could see both bags from behind the boxes and caught a glimpse of the men dressed in black outfits. She heard the door close, and shortly after, the engine started. Then she could feel the van in motion.

Gretchen felt that the van might have been in motion for about five minutes when she overheard one of the men mention "marshland at Dunkersfield." While she could hear them talking, she tried to slit holes into the bags with her scissors, to see what was inside, but her plan failed. The van came to a halt, so she quickly returned to her hiding place and prayed that she didn't get caught. A few minutes later, she felt the van moving again. Then she decided to take the chance to send Theo a text and pictures she took—of the two suspicious sacks.

"Heading to marshland at Dunkersfield, in black van with two suspicious men in black outfits, and probably other victims. Send the police!"

Gretchen noticed the time when she pressed SEND: 3:50 a.m. She returned to her place behind the box, feeling hopeless. It felt like the van had been moving for an hour before coming to another halt. She continued praying, hoping her dream would come true.

"Please, Father, do not turn me over to the tormentors of my soul or a pauper's grave. Instead, make for me a way of escape. Give us peace, courage, and strength to bear it, as Your will be done."

Then Gretchen heard Bertha's voice: "Think deeply. Follow the Creator's lead."

Shortly after, Gretchen heard the van's back door open, and the two men dragged out the crocus bag they had put in last and walked away. Gretchen decided to get out before they came back. They were gone for less than five minutes. It was still dark all around, and she had no clue where she was, but she stood behind a tree next to the van and prayed she wasn't seen. The men came back and took out the second bag. She was almost sobbing but quickly mustered the courage to think deeply. She had to figure how to remain undetected.

In the event she didn't make it back to Vanityville, Gretchen decided to send another text message to Theo:

"I will always love you."

Gretchen could hear the footsteps passing by the tree's huge trunk, which became her shield. She knew she had to stall the men until the police got there. Then she noticed a text from Theo.

"Follow your heart. I'll always love you too!"

Gretchen knew then that both her guardian angels were close by, and she had nothing to fear. So she came out from behind the sycamore tree and threw a rock at one of the van's windows. The men stopped and looked back. She waved her hands for them to see her, but just then, a police car pulled up with its lights flashing and sirens blaring. The men turned on their heels and ran the other way. Gretchen was surprised to see Bertha's bright, purple-red glow and her wings flapping.

Gretchen heard the police warn, "Stop, or we'll shoot!"

One of the men did not heed the warning. Instead, he fired at the police, who returned fire and shot him several times. During the crossfire, Gretchen took a picture of the van, the man going down, and the other man, who had raised his hands in surrender.

Gretchen believed that bodies of loved ones were dumped there in the marshland. She could see many crocus bags all around and picked up a couple of them. She got into one from her feet up to her waist. Then in a fetal position, she laid herself down under the sycamore tree, the other bag beneath her head.

By this time, several more police cars had showed up. After a while, all the flickering lights were gone, and she could only see Bertha's soft glow near her.

She hummed along with the tune she could hear in her mind:

Hmmmmmm, Hmmmmmm
Birds singing in the sycamore tree,
dream a little dream of me.
Hmmmmmm, Hmmmmmm

While I'm alone and blue as can be,
dream a little dream of me.
Hmmmmmm, Hmmmmmm
In your dream, whatever they be,
dream a little dream of me.

Minutes later, Gretchen heard Theo's voice calling her name.

Theo saw the purple top of a figure, looking like a mound at the base of the sycamore tree. He could hear his heart pounding as he got closer.

Drawing near to the tree, he could see that the mound was moving. Closer yet, he realized that the mound was a person, Gretchen, lying in the fetal position, in a brown crocus bag. Her face was covered with dust. She shielded her eyes from the glare of the light as he approached.

"Gretchen, what are you doing here?" he asked.

"Following the Creator's lead."

"Why are you inside a crocus bag?"

"They were apparently left here for me. I would rather the crocus bag to a pauper's grave. It's cheaper and allows me to breathe."

"Oh, my poor Gretchen. Come here," Theo said as he stooped to pick her up.

"No need to take me away. I belong here."

"No, you do not. You don't belong here. I'll take you back to my home; that's where you belong."

Theo set the flashlight down, its light radiating upward for him to see. He created a little bedding with a few crocus bags on which he sat Gretchen and propped her up into a sitting position against the sycamore trunk. Her purple dress soaked right through by the marshland muck around the sycamore tree. Theo wiped her face with some wet wipes he took from a plastic container in his backpack. He took off his black fleece jacket and put it around her, hugging her shivering, feverish body.

As he offered her sips of vitamin water from a bottle in his backpack, she said, "Yes, please take me to your home so I can take a shower and sleep a little. I promise that if I don't feel better, I'll allow you to take me to the hospital."

"You got it," said Theo.

As she took a couple more sips of water, they noticed the steady blue light of a firefly hovering around them. It came to land on Gretchen's shoulder. She rested her head on Theo's shoulder as he sat next to her and continued to feed her fluids. Gretchen pointed to the western sky, where several winged creatures were rising from the marshland and soaring into the sky.

"Look," she said. "The angels are soaring over there."

Theo could see the creatures, so he knew Gretchen was not delirious. Her head rested on his shoulder as they watched. He now believed what was written in the Bible: "He will give his angels charge over thee."[25]

"See that one with the purple-red glow, leading the way?"

"Ah, yes," said Theo, a little hesitant as he looked toward the heavens.

"You may be doubtful, but I believe that's our beloved Bertha, the brilliant one. I can recognize her glow from a million miles away. Colanda is behind Bertha, also in purple."

"Or it could be Phillis."

"I believe Bertha and Phillis are one and the same."

Gretchen and Theo could see other larger-winged creatures leading the way, as other souls with wings kept rising from the marshland. Amid the silence, Gretchen could hear the pounding of her heart as it got louder, and the angelic figures in the sky faded. She thought that she may never see Bertha again.

---

[25] Psalm 91:11.

Theo noticed that her eyes were closed and asked, "Are you okay?"

"At least you are here," she said, "so I should be okay."

Theo noticed she was warm to the touch and shivering; he assumed she was dehydrated and likely coming down with an infection.

"This place is extremely filthy," he said. "Maybe you should reconsider and allow me to call the ambulance."

"I'll get over this soon," she said. "All that matters now is to know that my mission has been accomplished."

Theo packed his bag and slung it on his back, picked up Gretchen in his arms, and walked back to his Bentley parked nearby. After driving an hour, they reached his house and went inside. Gretchen took a long, warm shower and was soon in bed and sound asleep.

The next morning, she woke up and went out to the living room, where Theo was sitting on the sectional. She lay down next to him, with her head on his lap. She was relieved to hear that all three suspects had been effectively neutralized. There would be no more oppression from them. She had dreamed about Oscar, Theo's attacker, the man he saw at Chuck's Place. The picture Gretchen had taken was very helpful to the police, connecting him to the scene. However, he was found dead in his cell, where apparently, he had hung himself.

Gretchen understood that all the events occurring in her dreams, in Gentry Cove, seemed so far from reality as she knew it during her real-life experiences. Yet when she woke to face evil in its most cruel forms, the reality to her was no different. The events in her dreams served to prepare her for handling those in real life and to reinforce her faith and trust in the Creator. *Resurrected Gentry Crossing Over*, depicting the raptured souls in Gretchen's dream, may never be validated in real time. Yet she believed wholeheartedly that the remains of numerous innocent souls might have been put to rest, dumped in marshlands such as

Dunkersfield. The poor, homeless, ignoble rejects were all God's creatures deserving of respect and fair treatment. Gretchen's dream of some soaring to greater heights with Bertha-Phillis leading the way was real. In time, dreams would come true to glorify the Creator.

Theo explained what had gone on. The part that Gretchen had missed in her dream was that Theo was taken to the hospital and treated for the stab wound to his right shoulder. She was surprised to hear that Glenda had confessed to sharing Bertha's medical record with Skip. Mattie had reported suspicions about Glenda's activities. Regarding the pictures Gretchen texted to Theo, he had released copies to the police. Leo had been declared missing. Whoever was in the other crocus bag was unknown. It was confirmed that Berba died of gunshot wounds and Butch was in jail, awaiting trial.

They heard the doorbell. Theo went to answer, and Officers Gabriel and Rafael were standing there; Officer Gabriel was holding Theo's camera. The policeman informed him that his camera was found at Dunkersfield marshland. The fish video helped them to track him as the owner, and to his surprise, it was undamaged.

When Gretchen joined Theo at the door, Officer Gabriel told her they appreciated her outstanding community service. A feeling of joy came over her as the officer reassured them that the neighbors were warned to stop taking pictures of the Worlingtons and their guests in the privacy of their home.

Theo was happy to get his camera back. He was extremely happy to hear that Gretchen's manuscript was almost completed; her mission was accomplished. Gretchen could hear the sadness in Theo's voice as he admitted to feeling okay with her coming and going, seeking refuge in Vanityville. He was aware that she had unfinished business back home and felt that they were inextricably bound.

"Take your time, my Li'l Pearl," Theo said. "I admire your

love for the Creator. Your passion for knowledge is immense, and my love for you is eternal. Whether I am white, black, or otherwise, in this or any other lifetime, I'll be there for you."

On October 27, Gretchen woke up when her alarm clock went off. The room was empty except for her laptop and the TV on a small table; the air mattress reminded her that she was back to more tyranny, in real time. She turned on the TV and began watching a tennis match from Paris. She thought it would be a good distraction, but only for a short while. Memories of Vanityville flooded her mind. She wept for a few minutes. Then thoughts of Theo cheered her up a bit. She was smiling as she recalled Theo singing along while he danced with her: "Or we may never meet again, but then it's not for me to say."

Gretchen's heart was overjoyed that Theodorus, her gift from God, had been there at a time when she needed him the most. She thanked him for being there for Bertha as well. Gretchen could truly say that meeting Theo was one of the greatest experiences of her life. Her connection with him had awakened some human qualities that had been dormant. His kind, angelic nature had brought out the very best in Gretchen. She believed wholeheartedly that he would be true to his words: "I am willing to cross over also. I have promised Punkey that I will never allow anyone to hurt you anymore."

Gretchen clearly heard Bertha's soft voice pleading, "Save the children."

In that moment, Gretchen realized that she had a couple more night seasons already carved out for her. Her greatest desire was to serve humanity and glorify the Creator. She hoped that *Resurrected Gentry Crossing Over* would bring redemption and go down in history, in memory of her soul mate Bertha, the superlative embodiment of Phillis. Sealed this day, December 5, 2018.

Chapter 13

Gretchen was not at all happy that her situation had not changed, except for the worse, when she was awake in real time. She would cry a lot, almost daily. Then she became resolute.

I must obey the urge to break the seal on my manuscript, she thought. *It would be very remiss of me not to give more detail of my ordeals in real time.*

She revealed that deep down, she was doubtful. After writing twelve chapters, dreaming of redemption for Bertha/Phillis, there seemed to be no real fulfillment. Yet the fear of her ending up in a pauper's grave was more real than before. She could be homeless at any moment, but no one seemed to care. Instead, disingenuous and uncaring individuals had been capitalizing on her vulnerability. The silence had intensified as the tyranny continued in her life. She was getting daily reminders about her past due payments on loans she'd been trying to pay off for more than ten years. The balances had increased over time as interests accrued. Her second term life insurance policy had lapsed, after she'd paid thousands of dollars (on two separate occasions, between 2010 and 2018).

She was still unemployed, with about fifty dollars in her accounts combined.

She had not worked since September 5, 2018; two months later, she was sent home on sabbatical from her humanitarian work, for which she was receiving a monthly stipend. She was not eligible for unemployment benefits.

She had a joyful look on her face when she opened an envelope that came the mail a week later. There was a food stamp card and a note: "You have $198 on your card." That would take her through the month of March. She felt thankful that her fifteen years of banking skills and self-discipline had taught her how to carefully manage her income, now a widow's mite. Yet she was very tearful that she couldn't pay her monthly living expenses, about $480, including dental insurance payment, which was two months past due. The only source of income she had was her deceased husband's annuity benefit (about $390 monthly). Suicide would have been a viable option, but for her faith. She had made it clear that she would never hurt herself or anyone, so no one had to worry about her.

Gretchen could feel herself clinging to Big Pearl—her overachieving alter ego who'd always engage with her in self-talks that nurtured her self-esteem. Gretchen had not heard from Bertha or Theo since December 5, 2018. *No fault of theirs,* she thought. *I wanted to concentrate on finding a real job.* She was told that a hospital needed someone to work in housekeeping, but the application process was lengthy, plus she was overqualified.

Gretchen had gone to the emergency room with complaint of chest pain, twice in the last twelve months. On both occasions, cardiac workups were negative, and she was relieved when all her lab results came back normal. She agreed, as the doctor explained, that her recurring chest pain and high blood pressures were related to stress. Gretchen's blood pressure readings were usually normal, on waking up and after returning from dream world.

Gretchen tried to focus on Big Pearl's encouragement.

You must try to relax and take it easy. Forget about work and people who don't care about you. They can hurt you only if you give them room inside your mind. Concentrate on what makes you happy and God will provide, Gretchen could hear her say.

I think I got my resilience, among other good traits, from you, Big Pearl, Gretchen thought.

Good. I'll always be here for you, whenever you need me.

It was obvious to Gretchen that she had been ripped from her career; the rejection was psychologically traumatic. Yet she always had a song her heart. Some of her favorites were "It Is Well with My Soul," "I Believe," "Take My Hand, Precious Lord," "If I Can Help Somebody," "You'll Never Walk Alone," and "Tears Are a Language God Understands." Gretchen would often sing or cry herself to sleep.

———◇———

On February 2, 2019, about eight o'clock at night, while sound asleep, Gretchen could feel herself spiraling downward. There was thick darkness all around her, and she could not see through it. Her mind was made up to wait it out, but her heart felt extreme sorrow that her mission had not been accomplished.

My soul cannot go to rest, she thought. *I must finish the final draft of my manuscript.*

She realized, however, that her journey downward had gotten darker. She panicked, thinking that she would never see the light again, and felt herself gasping for breath.

Then suddenly, Gretchen felt a jolt to her shoulder. She could hear Bertha's voice saying, "Li'l Pearl, you cannot go under for going over. Rise up."

Gretchen opened her eyes and saw a purple glow radiating from a figure at the left side of her bed. "My dear Bertha! I'm so glad you came, just in time. Thank you."

Gretchen was surprised that the purple glow was gone when she was fully awake. Yet she could hear Bertha's voice saying, "Be strong and have courage; do not be afraid of them. I will never leave you nor forsake you."[26]

Gretchen's chest tightness had subsided, and the light slowly

---

[26] Deuteronomy 31:6

reappeared, as it was before. She was happy that Bertha had showed up, just before she took her last breath, but sad to know she had left so quickly. Gretchen looked toward the direction of the voice and responded.

"Bertha, please show yourself to me. I thank the Creator for reconnecting us. I'd tried several times to return to Dreamersville, hoping to see you and Theo, but I couldn't find my way. There was darkness all around."

Gretchen kept staring at the light of the lamp on the coffee table and could hear herself saying, *Think deeply, and trust the Creator's lead.*

Gretchen realized that Bertha was wearing her purple T-shirt with "Resurrected Gentry" printed on the front. She was sitting at the coffee table, and her attention was fixed on Gretchen.

She continued thinking deeply and could see herself in her pink Resurrected Gentry T-shirt. She was sitting opposite to Bertha. Gretchen could feel the joy as she noticed the smile on Bertha's face.

"I wanted to share a bit of good news with you, after we parted in 2013, and you know how difficult it became."

Gretchen was happy to see Bertha nod in agreement, but sad when she noticed that she could not read the contents.

"It's written on that paper in your hand that your children have unconditional *jus soli,* which means the rights to the American soil."

Gretchen heard when Bertha corrected her. "*Our* children," she heard her say. "You had picked up the pieces where I left off."

Gretchen felt like she was in a trance that took her all the way back to 1784, when Phillis died in childbirth.

"I understand now," said Gretchen. "Our children's citizenship was sealed after the ratification of the Constitution in 1789 and the Bill of Rights in 1791, seven years after Phillis died. They have birthright citizenship, in accordance with the Convention on Human Rights. Did you hear that, Bertha? Our children are Americans by birth. We don't need to worry too much now."

"Only that we don't know where to find some of them," Gretchen heard Bertha say, "and that's why I need your help."

Gretchen noticed that Bertha was silent, her eyebrows furrowed as if trying to think. She could see the tears flowing down her face as she handed the paper back to her. Gretchen summed it up that Bertha was grieving, and she joined in with her.

"We'll find them, Bertha, and they too shall soar."

Gretchen and Bertha could hear the song "No Eyes Have Seen" playing in the background, and they joined in, singing the last line:

"But by His spirit, He has revealed His plan to those who love Him."

The next day, at twilight, Gretchen, in fuchsia and black, looked up from typing on her laptop and saw Theo, wearing his favorite pink shirt and jeans. He was seated in the chair across from her, at the coffee table.

"Theo, how did you get here?" she asked, looking utterly surprised.

"Sorry that I had to sneak up on you in your dream; my global positioning system picked up on Bertha's purple glow. Do you mind?"

"Not at all. I am excited," Gretchen replied as they got up and embraced each other. Their lips met, and Gretchen collapsed into Theo's arms.

"My Li'l Pearl, your daily cry for help and prayers for deliverance from evil were too much for me to bear. I could not watch while you get hurt. Besides, I need you too."

Gretchen was more stunned when she heard Theo's response.

"Theodorus, you are truly a gift of God. I thank you," she said.

"It's the least I can do. I wish the money I have in Vanityville could be used here. You would have it all, but don't lose hope."

"It does feel like I'm dreaming, but I'm truly happy to have my down-to-earth angel here with me."

"No better place to be, especially at such a time like this."

Gretchen could hear their hearts beating as one; she felt real joy and peace in that moment, knowing that the Creator had sent an angel to rescue her. She heard Theo say that he had put his wing ritual on hold to be at her side.

"Please, take me back with you. I don't want to stay here."

They could feel their warm bodies clinging to each other, and their hungry hearts yearned for each other's tender touch. Theo saw Gretchen's tears as an outpouring of great pain that only his love could heal. He prayed for God's mercy and grace for the full expression of his love, seeking to connect with hers. Her kiss was affirming.

Moments later, Gretchen could hear Theo complimenting her bed as he lay beside her.

"This air mattress is very strong. I'm very grateful for it."

Gretchen informed Theo of her visit yesterday with Bertha.

Then, she listened attentively as he updated her about some interesting events that occurred after she left Gentry Cove. A major one was that Theo managed to sell Colanda's house. Skip's legal representative was ordered by the court to remove the fraudulent lien from Colanda's property, and Theo ensured that all proceeds would go to Drake. Butch had escaped from a prison outside of Gentry Cove, where he was imprisoned for life for his involvement in Colanda's death. It was also revealed that Butch had helped his half-brother, Skip, to stage the death of their mother, so they could cash in on her life insurance policy. Gretchen was shocked to hear that Trent had died of a heart attack, and the new headmaster, an African American and newcomer to Gentry Cove, had been having difficulty adjusting.

"Most of the twelfth-graders in your English Lit class graduated and have gone to colleges out of state."

Theo handed Gretchen several letters; she opened the envelopes and read them. It warmed her heart to know that she was missed by all and would always be remembered for her respectful, selfless, and caring qualities.

"Remember when Katandria explained paradox? She said, 'Danielle, better known as Miss Gretchen, is my hero.'"

"I remember, but I must admit that I didn't understand what she meant."

"She meant that you'd saved those children."

Gretchen listened attentively as Theo explained, *"Resurrected Gentry* may be about the redemption of Bertha and Phillis, and the gross cruelty that had befallen you, but you'll come to understand how many more people in this world may identify with similar sufferings. Dunkersfield was where the bodies of poor people were dumped (like at Gehenna, in the valley of Hinnom, a place of sacrifice by fire).[27] Some migrant children who weren't successful to advance to paradise in Vanityville or gain rites of passage to heaven often disappeared. The majority of those migrant children with no parents or means of survival were at risk. Many had committed suicide or starved to death because they lacked real support systems in their lives," Theo reported. "It was for that reason I became the center's psychologist. You know the rest of my story."

"And what I've stumbled across in my dream may be only the tip of an iceberg."

"I agree. There is the greater unknown," Theo concurred.

Gretchen opened the thirteenth envelope and was moved to tears by the contents.

"Dear Miss Gretchen, I miss you so much and wish I had a mother like you. Thank you for taking the time to help me be more

---

[27] Joshua 18:16; Jeremiah 7:31

assertive and feel good about myself. The role I played as the judge in *The Merchant of Vanityville* made me realize how important it is to have a judicial system that treats people fairly. I want to be a judge when I grow up, and you are my inspiration and role model. Yours truly, Annabelle."

Theo explained that Annabelle was one of the students of the migrant families at the center. Those students' tuitions were paid for by grants, and the children gave back by entertaining Vanityville's citizens at events like the variety show. Many of those students moved on to be professional entertainers elsewhere; those who didn't, found odd jobs or returned to their native lands.

Gretchen was surprised but understood why she couldn't find her way back to Dreamersville Hotel. She felt sad when Theo told her that hotel was shut down and eventually burned down because dreamers were living fancy there and costing taxpayers too much money.

"I'm so sorry to hear that. I wonder what became of Bertha's belongings."

"We may never know, but she won't need them now," Theo said, as he chuckled, and Gretchen thought it was funny too.

"The marshland in Dunkersfield has been drained and replaced by cornfields. Those crocus bags you saw there have been burned. It's a good thing you got some gentry folk flying out of there when they had time," Theo reported.

"So you do believe that I wasn't delirious when you found me in Dunkersfield?"

"I believe. I'm still having flashbacks. It was awesome."

Gretchen believed that Bertha's constant cry to save the children was starting to make sense, and it should be taken seriously. Gretchen regretted having waited so long to take her seriously, only when she faced a similar doom. She felt Theo was reading her mind.

"Although I understand that the Creator is in control of your situation, you've been constantly disrespected and under surveillance daily. You've been suffering in silence while prominent organizations watch you lose your house to frauds. Your household items, some sentimental, are being auctioned, and your car sold for less than half its value. The worst was knowing that an attorney would charge you five thousand dollars as a retainer fee. It was also appalling that a nonprofit charity organization whose mission was to leave no veteran behind would deny you eligibility for their services because you are not homeless yet. Your dignity has been under fire, having to place your sensitive documents on public display. Most victims of identity theft, like you, are vulnerable, single women whose sensitive and personal information ends up on the dark web," Theo said.

Gretchen watched as he looked up to the sky, shook his head, and then continued, "I could not move on to heaven until some things got settled down here."

Theo realized he had spat out a mouthful, and Gretchen was the sponge. She cried, and he comforted her. After a moment's silence, he noticed that Gretchen had regained her composure and asked if she had any other questions.

"When did you arrive in Gentry Cove?"

"In August 1993."

Gretchen could hear her heart skip a beat. Then another beat when she heard the answer to her other question.

"Was Nate adopted?"

"By me, but he is Heather's son. I met them in 2001, when Nate was thirteen. Heather died in 2005."

Gretchen was speechless, and Theo could see that his response had an effect on her.

To shift focus and ease the tension, Theo asked pulled her close to him and kissed her on the forehead.

"Is that my favorite Red Door you're wearing?" he asked.

"Yes."

"How many times have you dated in twenty-six years?"

"Two. I'm sorry."

"No need to be," Theo reassured her with another kiss. Bringing her closer, he whispered, "Gretchen, I don't go to the mountain anymore. I'll return to Gentry Cove for my wings next weekend, then I'll be back."

"Congratulations," she said as they embraced.

Then Theo remarked, "I've realized that Heather and Punkey are butterflies. So you can't be Heather in fuchsia and black and I am white. Capisce?"

"Understood."

After another brief silence, Theo spoke.

"I am very happy with you. I'll be everything the Creator has carved me out to be, so which way should I go, baby?"

"Is that an Army thing?" Gretchen asked with a smirk.

Theo kissed her on the forehead and smiled. "You are simply wonderful," he said.

"You and I," Gretchen corrected him.

"And Bertha," they said in unison as they saw the dull purple glow.

Gretchen was reassured that they were inextricably bonded. It made them all feel happy.

Gretchen was starting to miss having Theo and Bertha around. It had been over twenty-four hours since they left for Theo's promotion to winged-angel status. She had been feeling a lot better and crying less, except tears of joy. She was super happy that her special guardian angels had crossed over. She recalled the memorable time when all three of them sat around her coffee table, Gretchen on the edge of her bed, watching Theo and Bertha blessing her manuscript.

On February 16, 2019, close to midnight, Gretchen was awakened by the feeling of something choking her. She struggled to free herself, but the grip got tighter. Something must have happened. She felt a sudden relief and opened her eyes. She could see a figure in red and black limping toward the back door, away from her bed.

Gretchen recalled Skip exiting the back door of the auditorium at the center. Then she was snapped back to earth, feeling dazed after another hit to her head. She was on the floor, between the coffee table and the mattress, and could hear a struggle. After a few seconds, Gretchen saw two hooded figures in black, out cold on the floor. She decided to stay still, playing dead, when she saw another hooded figure in black.

It pulled off its mask, and Gretchen could hear a voice say, "Butch, you devil."

Gretchen's heart was pounding at the sound of Theo's voice. She knew he was in danger, but she couldn't do much. Butch had a knife and was about to stab Theo.

Then she heard Butch respond, "I dreamt of this day, meeting you face to face; it sent me into an eternal nightmare."

Yet another voice, reminding her of Bertha, responded to Butch, "You shall see the light, but Heaven won't be there for you."

Gretchen could see the familiar purple glow—illuminating the room and knew that Bertha was on the warpath.

Butch looked at brilliant Bertha and asked, "What are you doing here?"

Then Gretchen replied, "What are you doing here? It's not your story or place to dream."

Gretchen had the metal stem of the lamp in her hand. She could see the surprised look on Butch's face as he turned to face her.

"You are making a mistake, bitc-"

"That's not my name, but I'll be the one to bid you farewell and enlighten the way to your eternal nightmare." She delivered a blow to his left temple as he raised his knife to stab her. She watched as he fell to the ground. "Bon voyage, from Bertha and Colanda," she exclaimed.

Shortly after, an ambulance and police car showed up;

Gretchen knew she was not in Gentry Cove, but her dream had not ended.

I shall decrease, so you can increase.

Gretchen knew that her time had come for a breakthrough, and she was ready. Bertha's spark was gone, but her guardian angel Theo was still there.

Gretchen and Theo watched as the police departed after they got the full story; they confirmed that Butch was the same individual who had escaped from prison outside of Gentry Cove. Theo walked over to Gretchen, and they embraced.

"Thank you, Dr. Mocktruman. May I be your patient? I have a malady that heaven won't cure. So I've come this far for your help. I've watched you at work and know you are the best."

"I'm sure heaven will wait. We have work to do."

"May we have some fun first?" Gretchen heard Theo ask.

Moments later, Gretchen felt like she was on a bird, like an eagle, soaring into the sky. She could see numerous angels surrounding her house. She was enjoying the panoramic view of Palm Beach when suddenly, she saw total darkness.

Then she heard a voice saying, "Don't look down, look ahead."

She obeyed and saw red and gold clouds, like the sun setting. The appearance was too overwhelming, so Gretchen closed her eyes again and began to think deeply.

The robotic voice sounded like Theo's, she thought, but she wasn't sure. Yet she realized it was no time to ask questions to distract the bird. Although she felt safe, a feeling of sadness came over her, thinking she had left earth and may never return to save the children.

Another voiced assured her that Bertha was not too far away. Gretchen was overjoyed to hear her sweet voice reminding her to trust the Creator's lead. Gretchen closed her eyes and relaxed, believing that she was soaring with Theo, and Bertha was leading the way.

———◇———

Shortly after, Gretchen woke up to find Theo sitting at the coffee table, reading an article he was preparing to publish. She was pleased to see him wearing a teal Resurrected Gentry T-shirt but concerned that he was lacking sleep.

"Do you ever sleep?" she asked.

"I do, but not while on duty," Theo said. "It's my job to keep watch, even when on earth. For the arrows fly by day and the pestilence walk in the darkness. Yet I'll cover you with my wings.[28] Hooded creatures are springing up, all around and seeking who they can devour."

For we wrestle against principalities, powers, rulers of the darkness of this world, against spiritual wickedness in high places,[29] she could hear Bertha echo.

Gretchen believed that the oneness she shared with Bertha and Theo might be perceived as an illusion, but to them, it was real.

"We are eternally bonded by the love of God, our heavenly Father, being joint heirs with Christ," Gretchen affirmed.

She understood that the reality of their oneness, like the invisible face of the Creator, cannot be known, but by virtue of their faith,[30] they believed. Gretchen recalled the words of a thinker who had put it succinctly: "Oneness is the great inferential. Is there something real beneath that illusion we call reality? For if oneness is not real and doesn't exist, then nothing is real, and nothing exists."[31]

Gretchen was very thankful for her guardian angels for such

---

[28] Psalm 91:4-6.

[29] Ephesians 6:12.

[30] Hebrew 11:3.

[31] Eisen (2003). *Oneness Perceived: A Window into Enlightenment.* https://www.academia.edu/522842/Oneness_Perceived_A_Window_Into_Enlightenment

a time as this. She was feeling a sense of urgency to embark on the next mission with Bertha and Theo: to save the children and bring more glory and honor to the Creator.

Gretchen could feel herself going off to a deep sleep again and was reassured that it would not be to a pauper's grave. *Resurrected Gentry Crossing Over* shall bring more redemption, awareness, and empowerment, despite the odds, moving forward. Affirmed this day, February 28, 2019.

Afterword

Gretchen's afterthoughts: This story became inevitable when I retreated, attempting to escape the bowels of dastardly hate and oppression. I was poised to celebrate my mountaintop experience, being at the pinnacle of a successful career, which I had rightfully earned. Yet, without notice, my feet were knocked from under me, and I instantaneously spiraled downward, hitting the proverbial rock bottom. For more than two years, I lay on my back, sleeping on the floor, in despair and at the lowest level of life, destitute and waiting in line for a pauper's grave.

There I met my alter ego, Big Pearl, who was also waiting in line. She was drawn into my world through divine connections that gave her the will to help me narrate our story. She was sequestered and blocked from earning a livelihood, a wickedness designed to drive her insane and to bury her in a pauper's grave. She became fully immersed in the bond of love with Bertha-Phillis, Theodorus (aka Theo), and me, reveling in unlimited powers,[32] according to the Creator's perfect and permissible will. It was clear to us that we had many things in common, but we did not take pleasure in talking about many of them. Perhaps time will tell. Yet we agreed that the constant grief we had to bear with Bertha might be erased by writing them out of our hearts and into the hearts that created them.

---

[32] John 1:12.

My story became our story because we shared a common bond; our love for the Creator and humanity made us inseparable. Evil trying to separate us only strengthened our bond of love and brought us peace. The Creator bestowed to us the support of seven archangels, for other forces to reckon with each day. I promised to write our story and pave the way for Bertha to soar. She emerged from death, defying the pauper's grave, and evolved into the Creator's guiding light, uplifting others who have forged ahead in silence. I concur with the author of our fate that we shall be more than overachievers, overcoming evil with love.

We have been severely punished for simply being passionate about honoring God with our lives. We were ripped from the people we love and never allowed to truly enjoy the fruits of our labor. We had put service before self and embraced the call to be servants with complete allegiance.

Despite the sufferings we endured throughout our entire lifespan, our goal was to glorify the Creator. We have redefined nobility as gentry with our blood, sweat, and tears. We shall all overcome the degradations of a pauper's grave, which only served to keep us enshrined/preserved for 265 years. Bertha, Theo, Big Pearl, and I have affirmed our sufferings for over twenty-five years. We strongly believe that the shackles of slavery, impoverishment, and depravity pale in comparison to the treasures that await us. The merciful, almighty Creator shall wipe away all tears. We have been persuaded that what was meant for evil shall be for our good and the Creator's glory.[33]

Our knowledge of *Gentry* goes back to the Encyclopedia Virginia, found in the public domain. In America, the gentry class was largely the richest men, tobacco planters of Virginia who relied heavily on indentured slave labor from Africa. In other terms, gentry was made up of nobility, aristocracy, and the Colonial social class of well-bred, upper-class individuals. Gentry

---

[33] Genesis 50:20.

also characterized people who were not members of nobility but had toiled hard and had genuine loyalty and sacrificial love for the universe and its people. From the 1500s to the 1700s, some slaves were freed because of their conversion to Christianity and allowed to own land, cattle, and even slaves. They earned titles of honor for their significant contribution to life.[34] In Thomas Jefferson's *Notes on the State of Virginia*,[35] he stated,

> Those who labor in the earth are the chosen people of God, if ever He had a chosen people, whose breasts He has made His peculiar deposit for substantial and genuine virtue. It is the focus in which He keeps alive that sacred fire which otherwise might escape from the face of the earth.

Nonetheless, some people of gentry status were deliberately ignored, robbed, abused, and mistreated by greedy, evil, selfish, mean-spirited people with no true sense of universal allegiance. It may seem bizarre that in desperation, we had to retreat into a dream world for our voices to be heard and for the world to be made aware of the cruelty and injustices we had to endure. At the point of hopelessness, being denied work (the most basic means for survival), we chose to seek refuge in the only means available to us: to write.

One by one, as *Resurrected Gentry Crossing Over* becomes real, so shall our dreams. Everything shall come full circle. We shall understand it better that freewill was not designed for abuse or to keep souls depraved for selfish gains. It is beyond sinful, abominable, and sacrilegious. Yet the Creator's amazing love is merciful and matchless. It is the only perspective that never fails to

---

[34] Tillson (2012). "Gentry in Colonial Virginia." http://www. EncyclopediaVirginia.org/Gentry_in_Colonial_Virginia.
[35] "Notes on the State of Virginia (1785)." www.encyclopediavirginia.org.

overcome hate. When the fullness of time has come, the Creator's kingdom shall come in this earth.[36] Every knee shall bow, and every tongue confess.[37] He who feels it shall know it is very true.

Our hearts were filled with joy when we saw Bertha soaring on wings, with other souls trailing behind her. Though it might seem weird, it was sublime to those who believed. Our visionary supporter, Theo, defied all odds in helping us to claim our heritage, redeem the innocent, and glorify the Creator. His Li'l Pearl would like to continue the mission: to serve humanity, be mother to the motherless, and heal broken hearts. By our beloved Bertha's words, "I will never leave you nor forsake you."

Together, we shall save the children and make their dreams come true. *Resurrected Gentry Crossing Over*, in this nightseason, is only the beginning. Greater work is yet to come.

These candles will burn out long before our passion ever will.

---

[36] Matthew 6:10.

[37] Philippians 2:10-11.